MAFIA CHRISTMAS VOWS
AN ARRANGED MARRIAGE SURPRISE PREGNANCY DARK ROMANCE

VIVY SKYS

Copyright © 2024 by VIVY SKYS

All rights reserved.

No part of this book may be reproduced in any form or by any electronic or mechanical means, including information storage and retrieval systems, without written permission from the author, except for the use of brief quotations in a book review.

MAGGIE

You know, if I squint and keep my headphones on, it looks festive out.

There's big flakes of snow drifting down from a cozy-looking grey sky. The air is crisp, and the little lights along the airport's runway look like Christmas lights, because they're blinking a very festive red and green, depending on what they're trying to do for the pilots.

If I try hard enough, I could definitely pretend that I'm back home in Des Moines. That I'm just heading home from college, and when I get there, my mom is going to have my favorite Christmas movie on and all the hot cocoa that I can drink waiting for me.

A stab of grief, however, shatters that illusion just as the announcements from the flight attendants blare in English and Russian over the speakers on the plane.

There is no house to go back to.

My mom is in hiding.

And apparently, the only reason I'm here is because my biological father made a deal with the devil to keep me from meeting the same fiery fate as the house.

The people around me jostle and grab their bags. Russian, thick and dark, flows around me in a river of words that I don't even come close to understanding.

I don't speak Russian.

Despite the fact that I'm evidently very much half-Russian.

"Miss?" the flight attendant blinks at me. I'm fairly sure that my father assigned her (or paid her, or bribed her, or whatever) to look after me. Since the second I got on this plane she's been watching me like a hawk.

And, I saw her texting someone earlier after taking a picture of me, so...

Yeah.

It's either that, or she's a member of the rival gang that's the whole reason I'm in this situation to begin with.

I sigh, grabbing my lone piece of luggage. "Yeah. I'm here. I'm guessing you want me to follow you?"

Her cheeks get a little red, but she nods.

"Well, let's get this over with," I mutter.

I follow the flight attendant and exit the plane.

We don't talk. But she somehow manages to stay with me through customs, where she takes the papers my sperm donor dad provided for me and does some fast-talking with the customs officer. He takes one look at my visa, and the color runs out of his face completely.

Great.

That's just freaking...

Great.

I mean, I know how he feels. I felt that way when I saw my biological father for the first time too.

"This way, please?" The flight attendant gestures toward the baggage area.

I follow her.

"Your bag?"

"Don't have one," I say, sighing.

She gives me a raised eyebrow, but I shrug. "Look, I didn't exactly have time to pack. This whole thing happened fast. Viktor... dad... just came to the apartment and..."

My jaws snap shut.

I don't know why I'm telling her this.

Heck, she probably already knows.

Maybe I just need to talk about it.

You probably do.

I'm like... partway to completing a degree to be a licensed psychologist. I like to talk about my feelings. I need to talk about my feelings.

Especially after having a bunch of men appear at my apartment, telling me that my mom is in hiding and that I need to come with them to safety.

Granted, it was about six months ago that the house burned down. So I've done my best with moving on from that.

The rest of it?

Still grappling with all of that.

The flight attendant doesn't make a comment, but gives me a bland smile instead.

"So," I say, shuffling awkwardly. "Do you work for my father, or..."

"No. I am with Mr. Orlov."

Ice creeps down my spine. "Oh," I murmur.

Her smile brightens. "Yes. Please. This way," she gestures to the airport exit.

My heart slams in my chest.

I wish I could call my mom. I did FaceTime with her, before I left. She seems fine. She assured me that she was okay, and that I should do whatever my bio dad was telling me to do.

I believed her.

Now, I wonder if maybe I shouldn't have.

"Miss?"

The flight attendant is staring at me.

I nod.

Meekly, I walk toward the airport exit.

You're here to stay safe. To keep you and your mom safe. You're here to keep them from coming for you.

It's the logic that I've been following this whole time. If I go through with this, if I do what my dad laid out for me, then we'll be safe.

No one will come to burn down our house. No one will follow me around campus. No one will hurt my mom.

Safe.

And if it means that I have to marry a stranger to do it, then so be it.

I haven't felt safe in months. Not since I saw the pictures of my childhood home on the news, reduced to ashes.

Not since my mom told me that she was trying to hide, and that she'd tell me more when she could.

Safety has been an illusion for a while now.

However, as I follow the flight attendant out of the airport, I wonder if I'm doing the right thing.

Because right now?

'Safe' is the last thing I feel.

One thing I've learned about Russia... it is really *really* freaking cold.

Even in my trusty Eddie Bauer puffer jacket, I'm shivering in the back of the car.

After the airport, the flight attendant brought me to a long black SUV. I got in, the panic that I felt at the airport intensified as the driver slammed on the accelerator, barely looking out at the world as he did.

Alarmingly, we almost hit not one, but two people on the way out.

I'm not sure why, but I definitely got the impression that the chauffeur is on a timeline.

However, I don't speak Russian, and my squeak of terror did nothing to change his mind, so I just did the best I could. I settled in and watched the sights as they zoomed by my window.

The city that I flew into started to fall away. Disappeared, actually.

It was swallowed by the snow as we sped away.

It's been a few hours since the airport, and I'm beginning to feel panic creeping back into the edges of my mind. The fact that I'm stuck in this tin can doesn't help either, and my senses are on overdrive as we keep moving through the night.

The inside of the car is so quiet, I can hear the individual flakes of snow pelting the windshield. The driver looks like he injects protein straight into his veins, and the leather seats smell like way too much cologne.

It's kind of nauseating.

I'm doing my best just to stay warm and stay alert.

I'm not doing well at either of those goals.

The overwhelming smell of the cologne is choking me, clawing at my throat, and the puffy coat that I'm zipped into isn't doing anything to keep me from feeling cold.

All in all, this sucks.

I tug my phone out of my pocket, turning it on. It's not my regular phone; my dad took that and smashed it before I left, giving me this one instead.

He insisted that it was for my own good. That whoever is hunting us, his enemies or whoever they are, could track me through my old phone.

This one has two numbers programmed in it. My mom, who I am supposed to text very sparingly, and my biological father.

I definitely ignore his number and go for my mom instead.

Me: Landed.

Mom: Oh thank god. I've been hoping to hear from you, Mini.

I smile. It's definitely her. My dad doesn't know the nickname, and we agreed on it before I left so we could verify communication.

Me: How's it going with the sperm donor?

Mom: Weird.

In the rushed hours before I left, my mom explained that my biological father was kind of a one-night stand situation. They were never married, and she met him when she was a cocktail waitress in a hotel in Vegas. She had no idea that he was part of a Russian mob until…

Well.

Until the house burned down.

Apparently though, she did have a mysterious amount of money that would appear in her bank account occasionally through the years. She assumed it was from a settlement that she'd been in for a car accident years before.

Whether I believe that or not is not the point. The truth is that somehow, my bio dad knew about me.

And was providing for both of us for a while.

Me: Well, keep holding on. At least you don't have to marry him?

I meant it to be a joke. I really did.

But my mom calls me, and I pick up.

"Hi," I murmur.

"Sweetheart, I'm so sorry," she says, tears thick in her throat. "You don't have to do this. Really, you don't. You say the word and..." her voice trails off.

I sigh.

"It's okay, mom. Really. It's fine. I mean it's not like I have much of a life as an alternative, right?"

I hear her choke on some tears, and know that was the wrong thing to say.

"Mom. I'm serious. I couldn't finish my degree if I was constantly running from some kind of rival mob or gang or whatever dad is into. And if you weren't safe..."

"You don't have to do this for me, baby."

"I know. It's my choice," I say firmly.

All of that is true.

When dear old dad explained what was at stake, he did it completely factually. He, Victor Igor Kozlov, had made an enemy years ago. The enemy was a very powerful guy, and he never told us what his name was. The enemy had gone through all of dad's connections, and then found us.

A woman he had a one-night stand with, and a daughter that resulted.

That apparently he'd been watching over.

For years.

He explained that he couldn't actually be part of my life because of said enemy. That he knew this guy would try to use all connections against him. So instead, he donated money to my mom, and apparently helped arrange a very serious string of what we thought was good luck. I always thought it was a little odd that things just seemed to go perfectly well for us... my mom bought a house on a very low income, all my schools were always best in class, I got into whatever college I wanted, etc.

We really did just think that it was good luck.

The fact that I did, in fact, have a dad who cared about me is not something I've had time to process. Because in the same breath, my father explained the only way to get this other mob member— who had discovered my mom and me— off our backs, was to make an alliance.

And the only way to make an alliance was to offer myself in marriage to Alexei Orlov.

He explained it like I had a choice.

However, given the facts, and the fact that his enemies had already burned my childhood home to the ground...

It wasn't really a choice.

I have no idea who Alexei Orlov is. He's not searchable on the internet. He lives in Russia, which isn't exactly a place with a ton of available information.

All I know is that in a situation where my mom and I are about to be torn apart by wolves, he's the thing that keeps the wolves at bay.

Marrying the bigger monster isn't exactly my idea of a great Christmas.

But, as the SUV speeds away into the Russian night, my resolve hardens.

My mom is the most important thing in the world to me. I'd do anything to keep her safe.

I tuck the phone against my chin and sigh. "It's going to be okay, mom. I love you. I have to go."

"Love you too, sweetie," she murmurs.

The phone call ends, and I look out into the darkness.

Telling her that everything is going to be okay is just reassurance. It's something I've done a dozen times, especially since agreeing to this plan.

I only wish I believed it was true.

ALEXEI

My phone has been buzzing through the entire meeting.

It's beginning to be annoying.

On the computer screen in front of me, my cousin Boris Novikov drones on. He's trying to propose something to do with a trade deal between the Irish and our collective network, but I'm barely paying attention.

One, Boris is an idiot. I have very little faith that he will actually make this happen, especially because he only recently came into his seat. His father, a distant uncle of mine, was killed in an explosion in Amsterdam, and Boris is simply not ready for this level of responsibility.

Two, my cousin Anastasia already has some inroads with the Irish. Stassi is another Novikov, although also a cousin to Boris. With the amount of Novikov's in our family tree, it's often impossible to tell how they're related. However, there's no doubt that the Orlov and Novikov families are connected.

And anyone who doesn't know will find out the hard way not to mess with either of us.

Which, I suppose, is why my phone is buzzing.

The Kozlov girl should have landed.

Your future wife.

The thought makes my lip curl.

I do not wish to marry a Kozlov. Even in my world, they're viewed as shady. Immoral. Difficult to make deals with, because they have been known to go back on their word. There was the whole thing in Belarus many months ago, and I'm still not happy with the fact that the Irish managed to kidnap my cousin. I hired a couple of Kozlov's as security, and they were supposed to be guarding her, but they failed. I killed them immediately, and buried them deep in the North Sea after their failure.

However, Igor Kozlov made a very compelling case to marry his daughter and form an alliance between our families.

He is a different Kozlov, only distantly related to the ones that I sent to sleep amongst the darkness of the sea. He has lived in America for quite some time. Made a very powerful enemy, one that I also count among my enemies.

He owes me, for the failures of his kin.

In addition, with the consolidation of the Rossi and De Luca families, and the fact that Benicio Souza is looking for a powerful heir to take over his empire...

Globalization is a bitch.

And I find myself in a position where I too must consolidate all resources that I can.

Plus, if I can remain married for one year, and produce a child to continue my bloodline, then I will have something that I deeply want.

An estate. One that has been in my family for a great deal of time. One currently sitting in trust, because for the first time in centuries, there is no Orlov guaranteed to inherit after me.

For the first time in centuries, it is at risk of being absorbed by the state.

Orlov House will not become property of the state.

I grit my teeth.

It did not survive multiple uprisings, simply to be absorbed into the government because I am unable to produce a family line.

Unfortunately, having a wife solves many problems for me.

But that still does not mean I wish to answer the buzzing from my phone.

"Is the Little Prince too good to provide input on this?" I hear Boris snap at me from the video call.

I focus my attention on the screen. *I'll fucking kill him.*

"Call me that again, cousin, and you'll have more holes than your financial model," I snarl.

A couple of other members of our family snicker, and Boris turns as red as the sunset. I lean back as another family member picks apart Boris' idiotic plan, pleased that I'm not the only one who sees through his moronic plans.

Eventually, the buzzing of the phone becomes too insistent. I sigh and click the call off, then pick up the phone.

Anatoly, my driver, is on the call.

"Boss," he mutters in Russian.

The girl must be around. "Yes?"

"The girl has no idea about any of this."

I tilt my head. "What do you mean?"

"She was just talking to her mother. I got the impression that not only was this not her choice, but she didn't even know Kozlov was her father until recently. Polina told me that she didn't even pack more than a coat, and she didn't bring a scrap of clothing other than what's on her body or what is in her backpack."

I sigh. I get the impression that Anatoly feels bad for her. "And?"

He pauses. "And, she has no idea what she's walking into."

"That is not my fault, Anatoly. I was not the one who decided to marry my child off for protection, and to atone for the sins of my kinsmen."

"The Kozlov you killed and the Kozlov sitting in this car are very different people."

I don't care. I simply don't. I require a wife for nothing more than the estate that's been in my family since the dawn of time, and no matter what he says, I'm not going to care about how she feels.

"How close are you to Orlov House?"

"Minutes," Anatoly rumbles.

"Good. See that she's settled."

"When will you be arriving?" he asks.

I sigh. I can tell that he's asking when I'll greet my bride-to-be, but I can't guarantee anything. "When my business in Novgorod is complete, Anatoly."

"She doesn't know anyone, boss. Doesn't even speak Russian."

"And that's the way it will stay," I bark.

Anatoly's silence makes a thread of guilt worm in my stomach.

"Get her settled. Keep her warm."

"Boss. It's almost Christmas."

A fact that has slipped my mind. The holiday is three weeks away, I note as I glance at the calendar.

"And?"

"She will be without family…"

"I don't give a fuck, Anatoly," I snap. "Let her decorate the house. Take her to get presents. Have her talk to her mother. She's here for a reason and I will hold her to that reason, but beyond that the girl is not my fucking problem."

"Boss," he murmurs, the words cold.

I sigh. "Get her settled. And Anatoly?"

"Yes?"

"Buy her some fucking clothes."

I meant what I said to Anatoly.

I don't care about having a wife. I never have.

My own mother died when I was barely a teenager. She was a wonderful person and I have a great deal of fond memories of her. She loved the holiday season, and often spent months decorating Orlov House, throwing elaborate parties for all my father's associates.

But those memories are mere fantasies.

Sometimes I think that they couldn't possibly have existed. Because my father?

He is nothing if not stern.

Not at all interested in celebrating holidays.

And would absolutely not marry someone who created the joy that my mother had around this time of year.

He taught me that there are things that matter more than a wife. Legacy. The ability to retain power.

Commanding respect through violence.

While they may not have been conventional, these were the things that made me far more suited for my current role than the ability to throw a merry party.

So I do not plan on returning to Orlov house.

Not, at least, until after the holiday.

Instead, I linger in my office in Novgorod. A day passes, the meetings that I am required to do go as planned, and I end my day by looking out over the lights of the city from my penthouse apartment. Ice clinks gently in my glass as I look out the window, the historical palaces illuminated at night. I can see snow drifting gently down, blurring the bright lights and softening their illumination, tempering the palace's shadows and angles into something kinder and smoother than the sharp contrast of light and darkness that I've grown used to.

It changes the environment entirely. No longer are the walls of the palace brutally bone-white, but they seem... pleasant.

The view is old, but it never fails to charm me. It's more than just the view, I muse as I sip my drink. Novgorod is an old town, one that has a pedigree going back as far as my own bloodline. Nobility, Russian and otherwise, have called it home for a great deal of time.

My own family, of course, counts themselves among them.

A family of direct descendants that have passed Orlov House and the surrounding estate down for hundreds of years. Father to son. Genetic link to genetic link.

I would be a fool to be the one who violates the legacy of this place.

More than that, I will not be the one who loses their ancestral home, all because he simply cannot be bothered to find a wife. Having one fall in my lap?

A perfect solution.

However, having a wife does not mean that I have to interact with said wife, outside of the duty required of me to provide an heir.

My phone buzzes and I look down.

Elena. The housekeeper.

The only woman who has known me since my own childhood. Who raised me after my mother's death.

Who often takes liberties she should not when it comes to our relationship... and yet I allow her to do it anyway.

Guilt wiggles into my stomach, but I open the phone.

Elena: Young man. The girl is lonely and sad.

Me: Comfort her.

Elena: She longs for her husband to come and meet her.

Me: I'm busy.

Elena: Did I raise you to be such a hard-hearted man? Oh, what have I done?. My poor heart. You do not know the depth of my sorrow, seeing you turn out to be such an icy, cold, callous...

I place the phone face down while her words continue to flow onto the page. Finally I sigh, denying her the pleasure of reading the long paragraph of words that are still scrolling through her text.

Me: Fine. I will come home.

Elena: Oh, my sweet boy. I knew you were not as hard-hearted as you believe. I will make your favorite for dinner, and I will tell the girl the joyous news.

My nostrils flare as I put the phone down.

I don't want to go back to Orlov House before the holidays. The memories are too thick. I will choke on them. However, the other option is to stay here, in the penthouse in Novgorod.

The snow falling outside creates a sense of isolation. The darkness and silence in the house makes it feel even more so.

Loneliness, pinched and pointed, stabs into my heart.

Sighing, I grab my computer. If I am to return to Orlov House, I will do so for a short time. I have too much going on at the moment to bother entertaining a simpering American woman, who is more likely to freeze in the Russian weather than she is to give me what I want.

Perhaps agreeing to take her as a wife was a poor choice indeed.

However, I am not interested in hunting for a wife. Having one fall into my lap was too convenient, and I will not turn her and everything she represents aside just because of my own discomfort.

I will not be the one who ends the legacy, and I will not lose Orlov House.

A few days. Just to settle her in. Just to ease Elena's guilt. Then, you can return.

Spending Christmas alone is not new to me.

In fact, I relish it.

The idea of facing a holiday in Orlov House?

That, I cannot do.

MAGGIE

Three days.

That's how long I've been sitting in this giant-ass house. Alone. Well, not entirely alone. The housekeeper and the other staff have been really, really nice. Elena in particular has been awesome. She speaks English, if a little haltingly, but she reminds me of like... an angry grandmother.

She's definitely Russian. No doubts about that. I've been bullied into eating beet soup and wearing about a dozen thick layers of clothing, even though I'm definitely not that cold.

The soup was kind of good, though. I won't deny that.

However, it's been three days and I have no idea what my future husband, or fiancé, or whatever he is, even looks like.

The house is covered in pictures. But they're mostly portraits of like... people who are definitely long dead. Today, I've decided to go around and look at all of them, and try to figure out who they are.

I'm in the second room of my journey, staring up at a particularly sour-faced woman, when Elena finds me.

"I brought you tea," she says, her voice making it clear that she will not accept any other option except accepting the tea.

I take it from her with a smile and sip. I'm definitely a tea person, and this stuff is addicting. "It's strong," I murmur, breathing in the heavy, smoky scent of it.

"Yes. Russian tea must get us through the Russian winter, after all," Elena says kindly.

I shiver.

"Who is that?" I ask, changing the subject as I sip my tea.

"I believe the current prince's great-grandmother," Elena replies, her brow wrinkled in concentration.

I pause. "Prince?"

She shrugs. "It is not the same as you might think. Orlov House, and the family of Orlov, are old. Very, very old. When Russia was not so much one place but many, they ruled over their small land here completely. Through many generations and revolutions, the title and the lands stuck, even if the meaning has changed."

"So... is he a prince?"

"In the oldest sense of the word, yes. But do not forget... many Russians have held higher titles, and in the modern world, it does not matter so much."

Huh.

"Anyway. He is a good boy, our Alexei. You'll see," she says, patting me lightly on the hand.

VIVY SKYS

The way she's talking him up, I'm pretty sure Alexei is not at all a good boy.

And, given the fact that he hasn't come home to greet his future wife, I'd say it's all but confirmed that he's kind of a dick.

Still, Elena is really nice. She's been nothing but kind to me since I arrived. She's firm, but radiates a kind of genuine care that I think is really hard to find these days.

So instead of pointing out that the guy seems like a real asshole, I nod. "I'm excited to meet him," I whisper.

If Elena can tell I'm lying, she doesn't give any indication.

"Come," she says, tugging on my elbow. "Let's go see the rest of the Orlovs. Might as well get to know the whole family."

Meekly, I follow her into the hall.

By the time Elena has introduced me to the portraits of every known Orlov since about the year 1300, I'm not only exhausted but have so many Russian names floating around my head, I'm beginning to feel dizzy.

"Thanks so much for the tour," I finally manage to grit out, squinting at Elena.

She beams. "Of course. Anytime."

"If it's okay with you, I think I'm going to go back to my room and take a nap."

"Anything, dochka," she winks at me.

I turn in the hallway. "Oh. Um…" I hesitate. Orlov House is enormous, and we just went through the whole thing, so I have no idea where I am.

As usual, Elena seems to know exactly what I need. "Head back down this hall. Turn left, then the next right. You'll go up some stairs and then your room is the first one on the right."

I give her a little half-smile. "Thanks, Elena. I'll see you for dinner."

"You will, dochka. It will be a very special dinner," she chuckles.

That sounds somewhat ominous. But, it could be just the usual Elena murmurings. She's a little dramatic, which I've learned since arriving here.

I brush it off and head out along the long trek back to my room.

I'll probably call my mom when I get there. We've talked every day since I got to Orlov House, and I'm beginning to think that things are actually going to be… okay.

As long as your asshole husband doesn't show up to ruin it.

Hmm. Maybe I don't want him to come from wherever he is. I don't think we've gotten married yet, but I actually don't know. Can you marry someone in Russia without them being present?

What if I never meet him?

What if my whole life is this house, and Elena, and…

I pause.

I'm so lost in my thoughts, I realize something very important.

I have no idea where I am.

Nor do I remember any of Elena's instructions.

Shit.

I spin around. The hallways of the house are beautiful, just like everything here. It's honestly something out of a movie; every detail is meticulously made, every single component of the walls are perfectly placed. Even the little bits of wood around the door frame look dressy, and if you get closer, you can see a tiny carved pattern of leaves, like someone etched vines into the wood.

It's all stunning.

"Get a grip, Mags," I murmur. "She said left down this hall, right down the next? Or right down this hall?"

My words are small in the empty space.

Shit.

Aimlessly, I push a door open.

When it creaks, I peer inside.

Oh wow.

It's another stunning room. This one, though, has a ton of furniture that's covered up by draped cloth. It's dusty; people haven't been in here for a while. However, the room's status is less important to me, because there's another stunning feature.

The windows.

Entranced, I pad across the soft rugs, drawn to the windows.

When I get there, I press my fingertips lightly against them. They're huge. Floor-to-ceiling, a massive panel of glass that had to have cost a ransom when they were installed back in the day.

Heck, they'd cost a lot today.

My breath fogs against the glass. You can see all of the grounds of the house from here. Everything is covered in a light dusting of snow, which is slowly drifting down from the grey sky, but the overall impression is...

"Stunning," I breathe.

The view is so beautiful, I don't notice when someone else enters the room.

A harsh voice rings out, and I jump, turning quickly.

"Who the fuck let you in here?" I hear.

Trembling, I turn.

My eyes widen.

Standing in the doorway of the room is the most handsome man I've ever seen.

And he's staring at me with eyes that burn with pure, unfettered rage.

ALEXEI

Who the fuck let her into my mother's rooms?

It's the only thing that I can think. I arrived from Novgorod not half an hour ago. No one was at the front door to greet me, which I found more than a little annoying. I stomped through the house, determined to figure out where everyone was, and that's when I saw my mother's door open.

A door that I personally ordered to be shut, and never opened, nearly a decade ago.

When I saw *her* against the window, her silhouette dark against the brightness of the snow outside, it took me a minute to register that I wasn't looking at a ghost.

It didn't take too long.

My mother was tall, willowy. The person standing in the window isn't. She's short, with a riot of dark hair that curls around her face and picks up light, forming kind of a halo that I'm stuck on. Her curvy figure makes my fingers itch, and I want nothing more than to reach out and wrap my hands around the lush landscape of her hips, not to mention the dip between her ribs and her ass...

What the hell? Who is she? What is she doing here?

"Who the fuck let you in here?" I snarl at her.

It's obvious that this is her. The American girl. I know every member of my household, so there's no one else who could be here.

In my mother's room.

Looking out the windows that she loved.

The memories of her are so crisp for me here, it's almost painful to look around the room.

And she just... walked in.

Like she fucking owns the place.

"I... sorry... I didn't know..." the girl says.

Her voice is nice. Her English is coated in that atrocious American twang that I can't seem to escape these days, but the softness of her words and the richness of her tone makes something in my chest tighten.

"You didn't know," I deadpan.

"No. I mean. How could I possibly have known? I just came in here because I got lost."

"You got lost," I repeat.

She huffs. "Well yeah of course I got lost! This house is freaking huge. Elena was showing me the portraits and all of that shit and then I wanted to go back to my room to call my mom and then..." her voice trails off.

I arch an eyebrow. "Do go on."

"No."

"Why not?"

She gulps.

"You're him, aren't you?

The tremble of fear in her voice makes guilt punch into my stomach.

Clearly, someone's been talking about me.

And they've given an accurate description.

"I don't know who you think I am," I murmur.

She gulps.

"Alexei."

I'm going to hell.

The way her pretty red lips part around my name puts my mind into a million dark, depraved places.

The rich tone of her voice makes my name hang in the air between us. She's waiting on confirmation; I'm just savoring the way my name sounds from her lips.

Well.

If she's waiting on confirmation, I might as well give it to her.

"Yes," I murmur.

It's more of a growl, I guess. I can't help it. My mind is still stuck on the way she said my name, and a primal part of me wants to know how I get her to say it again.

She's your wife. You can make her say your name whenever you want.

The thought hits me like a drug.

She's your wife.

Well.

Not yet.

"Oh," she says, her lips making the most perfect shape against her pale skin. "I... um... I'm Maggie."

Maggie.

We stare at each other.

I don't know what to do now. I hadn't thought this far ahead, and now that I'm staring at her standing in my mother's rooms, I simply don't know what I should do.

She's blinking at me, her beautiful face still backlit by the winter sky.

Maggie takes a step forward, her feet skimming the carpet of my mother's bedroom. My eyes follow it, noticing the dark stain near her toes.

Blood.

My mother's blood.

Just like that, any amiability wipes itself from my memory.

"You shouldn't be here," I growl.

Maggie pales. "I...um... like in Russia?"

"Here. In these rooms. Leave," I snarl at her.

She takes a hesitant step forward.

"Now!"

Maggie's feet scurry along the carpet. She brushes past me, and I catch the slightest whiff of something tantalizingly floral as she rushes by.

I grab the door and slam it closed, the woodwork around the doorframe shaking as I do.

Chest heaving, I look at her.

Maggie's eyes are wide. Her face is pale in the dim light of the hall.

She's afraid.

Of me.

"You can never come to these rooms," I say, my voice still deep. "Never again. Do you understand?"

"I..."

I don't wait to hear her response.

I storm down the hallway, leaving my soon-to-be wife behind.

I drink vodka in my study until the light disappears around me.

The staff creep quietly by. I pretend not to notice their hushed whispers in the hallway, or the fact that Elena has been hovering by the doorway for the last hour or so.

I'm Russian. Vodka is practically part of my blood. So the fact that I've been consuming it like water all day means I'm not drunk in the slightest.

Elena knocks, and I struggle to my feet.

Well.

Maybe I am *slightly* buzzed.

I open the door. "What?" I bark.

She bustles in past me, and even in the darkness I can feel her eyes on me. "You smell like you're a pig," she says.

"Good to see you too, Elena."

"Well it would be good to see you if it was not so terrible!" she turns, her hands on her hips.

I glare at her.

"You scared the girl," Elena says accusingly.

"She was where she shouldn't have been."

"She was in her house."

"It's not her house yet!" I snap.

Elena raises her eyebrows and turns to snap on a light. The brightness makes me flinch, and she makes a small, disapproving sound. "It will be her house. Or is she free to go back to America?"

I open my mouth.

Shut it.

Elena nods. "That is what I thought."

"It's not like that," I growl at her.

"Oh, it very much is. She's a nice girl. You'll see."

"It doesn't matter how nice she is, Elena. I am too busy to have a wife, but I need one..."

"For the house. Of course I know."

I arch my eyebrows at her.

Elena sighs. "You are a good boy, Alexei. You deserve to be happy."

"I am happy," I reply. Even as I say them, though, I know that they are a lie. That is surprising to me: I had never thought of myself as happy or unhappy.

I had only thought of myself as successful. Powerful.

But happiness?

It has nothing to do with the way I measure my life.

She pauses, and I can tell she wants to say something.

I know what it is.

But I refuse to listen.

"We'll draw up the papers tomorrow. Then she will be married to me," I finally grit out.

Elena's lips purse.

I turn, hoping she will take my hint.

With a sigh, Elena leaves the room. She pauses in the doorway. "And then will it be fine for her to walk in her own house."

I look away.

"Not that room, Elena," I murmur.

With a sigh, she leaves.

As the snow falls, I shut my eyes and let the vodka burn through me.

I do not need a companion, a friend, or a lover.

I need a wife.

Or my legacy will be lost.

MAGGIE

Many little girls dream of a wedding day. You know. The whole true love, marry the man of your dreams, live happily ever after thing.

I never did. Not really. I didn't have other dreams, per se, I just didn't think about it. My mom lived her life rather happily unmarried, and I just assumed that I would do the same.

Being a therapist, or a social worker, or both, mattered to me a whole lot more.

Well. Being productive and making myself part of the world.

I mean, being in love sounded *nice*, but it wasn't something I dreamed of.

And I definitely did not think it would happen like this.

I thought that Russia was kind of a religious place, but the ceremony seemed pretty darn agnostic. I repeated a bunch of words, which Elena translated for me quietly and quickly behind my shoulder, and before I knew it Alexei and I were married.

Afterwards, Elena, the priest, Alexei and I were alone in the room where the ceremony had happened.

Alexei had a glass of vodka, and was doing his best to mainline it straight into his veins. Elena and the priest chatted softly in Russian, and she gently ushered him to the door.

She cast a meaningful glance at Alexei, and barked something at him, then left.

I looked away.

The room's silence felt deafening.

"She told me not to move," Alexei said softly.

I blinked, glancing over at him.

"The priest is worried about the storm. Elena agreed that he should get moving, or he'd have to spend the rest of the day at Orlov House until the storm lifted."

"Oh," I say softly.

Alexei pulls out his phone and looks at it, then snorts. "The weather doesn't call for anything so dramatic. No one will be stranded anywhere."

"Why were they worried?"

The very corner of his lips pulls into a smile. "Elena said her knees hurt, and the priest agreed that the storm was pulling on his back."

"That happens to my mom too," I murmur, my lips curling slightly.

Alexei looks at me.

I look down at my hands. "When the weather changes, or when there's a big storm, she always says that her hip hurts."

"I guess that's one benefit of getting older. You can predict the weather," he says.

"Yeah. Well. I guess we'll find out."

I meant it in the sense that we'd just said vows. Granted, they were in Russian, but they can't be all that different than when they're said in English. For better or for worse, as long as we both shall live, is kind of part of the whole thing.

Alexei, however, seems to interpret my attempt at a joke very poorly. He makes a snarly noise in his voice and downs the rest of the vodka in one gulp.

Great.

I'm married to a man I don't know anything about, and I have pissed him off.

Again.

I tuck myself close, my hands wrapping around my elbows.

The silence is thick again.

"Your mother. Is she... she should be here," Alexei says.

My head snaps up, and I stare.

He's looking at me, his eyes studying me. He's intense. I realize that I've been spending so much time *not* looking at Alexei, that I don't actually know what my new husband looks like.

So I take the opportunity to look.

He's beautiful. He really is. Sapphire-blue eyes in a face that's sculpted from marble. Dark blonde hair that contains glimmers of lightness, which catch the faint glimmers of muted snowy light from the windows.

He's tall. His shoulders are wide, and underneath his dress shirt, I can see the flex of his chest and shoulder muscles.

If I had to conjure myself a husband, I'd be happy with how this one looks, for sure.

One of his eyebrows twitches. "Or, are you happy to not have her here?"

"No. I mean. I'm not sure," I say.

Alexei tilts his head again.

"I love my mom. She's all I have in the world. She's the reason I'm here," I huff.

"She is?"

I narrow my eyes and look at him. "Why do you think I agreed to this?"

"I have no idea, Magdalena."

The sound of my full name makes me sit up straight. "It's Maggie."

"I bet you let those familiar with you call you Maggie."

"I do."

"Then it seems appropriate for me to use Magdalena."

"Wow. So this is it? Strangers, even though we just got married?"

He tilts his head. "You were telling me why you agreed to this."

My heart breaks a little at the fact that he doesn't insist that we aren't strangers.

But I continue.

"The... mob. The ones who aren't you. They came for us, six months ago after they found out that my... biological dad apparently did really care about us. Burned our house down. My mom, she almost died," I whisper.

Alexei doesn't move.

"My parents weren't together. I was the product of a one-night stand. But evidently my bio dad, he was... helping. He sent us money. He helped get me into school. He cared about us enough that we could be used against him."

"And so when he offered to marry you off..."

I shrug. "I agreed. Because you're the bigger monster. Right?" I raise my eyebrow.

Alexei's face darkens. "I am."

"Well. I figured I could face a big monster if it meant my mom could be safe."

"Are you safe?"

I look at him.

"I heard you speak of your mother. Your father. Your desire to make sure that she is safe. But what about you? Did you not think yourself safe?"

"Well, I kind of figured the man who spent my whole life watching over my mom and me from afar wouldn't completely screw me over."

"You trusted a man you barely knew?"

Well, I guess when he says it like that... "Yeah. I guess I did."

"Magdalena."

I look up.

Alexei moves. I'm sitting on an overly stiff couch, and before I realize it, he's within about six inches of me. I lean back, keeping my eyes trained on his, as he looms over me.

"I am the bigger monster. Your father did not lead you astray."

"Okay," I whisper.

Something seems to flit across his face. He steps back, looking out the window to the snow falling outside.

"You are my wife now. You will live in Orlov House. If you'd like... we can send for your mother."

I blink.

"I am a monster. You must remember this."

"Alexei..."

He flinches.

I take a deep breath. "I know why I agreed to this. But why did you?"

He turns.

"If you're the one people are afraid of, then why did you agree to marry me? What do you get out of it?"

I'm genuinely curious. He's so hellbent on being seen as someone harsh, and cruel, but I've seen the way Elena frets over him.

I've seen how much she cares.

Elena is a nice person, and she wouldn't invest so much into a man who was truly a monster.

Alexei looks at me.

"There's no point in lying. I was honest with you. Might as well be honest with me too," I point out.

Alexei's perfect lips twitch again. "Fair point."

He shifts, so that he's sitting next to me. The couch is stiff as a board, and it doesn't give at all as Alexei sinks into it.

"My family is old," he begins.

I raise an eyebrow. "Elena called you a prince."

He nods. "In the oldest sense. The land, this house, they have been part of it for generations. I cannot inherit the house without a family. Without a wife," he says meaningfully.

Ah. "That's old school."

His lips tip again. "Old school," he murmurs, like he's never heard the phrase before. "Yes. Well. That is the case. I needed a wife, and I do not... this was a very easy way to get one."

"Don't date much?"

Alexei shakes his head. "No."

Well. That's interesting, at least.

Still, I had hoped that he was... I don't know. Interested in me, somehow.

That it wasn't quite as sanitized as it seems.

"I won't hurt you, Magdalena. I will protect you. I will protect your mother. I will keep you safe. Orlov House, the land, the staff... they are yours. We can keep your mother here. Any... I can give you money, and clothes, and anything you want, it will be yours."

"And if what I wanted was a loving family? A happy husband?"

Alexei looks away.

"Got it," I murmur.

"I will not promise something I cannot give," he says softly.

Well. At least he's being honest.

I stand.

"Where are you going?" Alexei asks.

Turning, I look back at him.

"Does it matter?"

"Elena will return. She wished to bring us cake."

That earns a little smile from me. "And you don't want to disappoint Elena, do you?"

Alexei nods. "She is... hopeful."

"For what?"

"That I am not the monster that I am."

Interesting. "And you want to give her hope, but not me?"

Alexei frowns.

I sigh, and settle back onto the couch.

Alexei looks at me. "What are you doing?"

"I like Elena. I appreciate your honesty. So I'll happily eat cake with her and pretend. What about you?"

Alexei takes a deep breath. I can smell his cologne, spicy and vaguely citrus against my senses.

"For Elena, we can pretend."

❋

The next morning, Alexei is gone.

I pretend it doesn't bother me. Elena lets me know that he's gone back to Novgorod for business.

He left me a black credit card, which I know from my general understanding of the world is the type without a limit.

Well, at least he wasn't kidding about the money stuff.

I spend the morning making the best of my unlimited money. Elena gives me the shipping address for the house, and I type it in so many times, it's basically memorized by the time I'm ready to talk to my mom.

When her face pops up on my screen, I do my best to smile.

However, she is still my mom, and the second she sees me her eyebrows pinch with worry.

"Oh, baby. What's wrong?"

Tears pinch the corners of my eyes.

I could tell her. I could explain everything, and let her know that I'm sad and lonely and nothing really seems right.

But...

I don't want her to worry.

"Oh, nothing. Just dusty in here and I've been sneezing a lot."

"You sure?"

I nod.

"Ok. Well, tell me everything."

I break a smile.

And then I lie through my teeth.

I tell my mom that we're planning a wedding later, and that she can come. I say that Alexei is kind, and thoughtful, and that he took me shopping. I tell her about Elena (which is true) and that the house is fantastic (also true). By the end of my story, I'm out of breath and half in love with the life that I've been describing to her.

It sounds lovely.

"Oh sweetheart. That sounds amazing. I can't wait to meet him!"

"I can't wait either," I say, my jaw clicking around the lie.

"So, what are you two doing for Christmas?"

I squeeze my eyes shut. "Oh, you know. Decorating soon, but since it's the first holiday I'm in the house and in Russia, I want to do like... Russian things."

"Well that sounds fun, sweetheart. I can't wait to see what you come up with."

"How's... um... dad?" I stumble. It feels weird to call him that but... technically he is my dad.

A blush creeps across my mom's cheeks. "Well, it turns out that I remembered your father to be a very nice man and... he's still a very nice man."

"Mom!" I say, genuinely smiling.

"It's been nice to reconnect, that's all."

Gross. "I don't know what you mean by that, and I don't want to."

My mom laughs. "I'm so happy you're doing well, sweetie. You know, maybe there's a silver lining to all this."

"Like what?"

She smiles. "Like, maybe we were meant to find these very nice men."

Oh god.

My heart crumples. "Hey mom, I gotta go."

"Okay. Love you, sweetie. Send me pictures of your decorating."

"I will."

I hang up the call, then stand up. I trot down from my room, making the long trek to the kitchen.

Elena is humming to herself, and I knock softly.

"Yes?"

"Are there any Christmas decorations in this house?" I ask.

Elena's eyes glint with something that's a little mischievous. "Why do you ask?"

Resolve grips me. "I'm the lady of the house now, right?"

"Yes you are, dochka."

I give her a nod. "Then I'd say, it's time to get this house Christmas-ready."

ALEXEI

❄

I fully intended to spend the rest of the year in Novgorod. I'm married. I've met my bride. I've celebrated with Elena.

There is no reason for me to go back.

But through the day, I find my mind returning to her.

Magdalena... *Maggie*... she is beautiful.

I won't deny that.

Petite. Lushly curved. Big, brown eyes that are large in her beautiful face. I looked into her, something that I had previously not done, and learned that she is smart as well.

She was going to school to become a doctor. Of the mind. A shrink.

I don't understand why, but I admire that she decided to make that decision.

I'm curious to know why her father chose to remain some kind of nameless benefactor. It seems to me that a man of honor and power would choose to protect his family by keeping them close.

But I wonder what kept him apart.

Magdalena's words ring in my ears. *You're the bigger monster.*

I have never been ashamed of being a monster. Not once.

I'm not ashamed of it now.

But I am... wondering.

Is that all she sees me as? A beast that can guard her? One who might bite, but she chooses to risk the teeth over the horrors that face her in other ways?

That does not sit well with me. Not at all.

I continue to ponder this predicament through the meetings of my day. When it comes time to retire to the penthouse, I call my driver instead.

Anatoly answers. "Boss."

"Take me to Orlov House."

He pauses. "The weather..."

"Are you a fucking mouse, Anatoly? You wish to hide so the snow doesn't bury you?"

Anatoly growls. "I will meet you in five."

I hang up the phone.

Anatoly doesn't need to make me second guess my choice. I want to be out of here, and I don't want to be in Novgorod.

I have the strangest compulsion to be at Orlov House.

And I am concerned that it has something to do with the newest inhabitant.

※

The snow is thick, and even I will admit that. Despite the SUV's tires and drive system, we slide the majority of the way back to Orlov House, and when we pull into the long drive, the front of the vehicle pushes snow in front of it.

Anatoly looks at me. "If the snow increases, I will not be able to take you back to Novgorod."

"We can take the tank," I rumble.

"It's still being serviced. And you'd use a tank to get back to Novgorod?"

If I need to escape, I will take any avenue that I need to.

"Boss," Anatoly sighs. "I'll take you wherever you need. You know this."

"Stop complaining about it, then."

He doesn't answer.

Safely parked in the garage, I slam the car door shut and march into the house.

The first thing I notice is the scent.

It kicks me in my chest. My mother used to make the house smell like this around the holiday season. Spices, citrus, and something sweet all grab my chest and pull at my heart.

I shut my eyes for a second, overwhelmed by the nostalgia of it.

It is the music next. Orlov House is a large home. Parts of it are old, but most of it is built as a manor house in the style popular in the 1800s.

Which means that it is a house of many hallways, many rooms, and very few large spaces.

The trill of music, melodies that seem bright, with all the singing in English, pulls me through the house. Hallway after hallway, room after room, everything looks...

Bright.

Finally, I find the source of the music. Gathered in the great hall, the living room where my mother loved to host her holiday gatherings, I find Elena and Magdalena.

And, surrounding them, are memories that I would rather have never faced.

My jaw drops.

Holiday decorations drip from every surface. Most of them are familiar; my mother had them, and I've seen them before.

However, they are in different locations than I remember. Or they are positioned differently. Or there are some that I don't remember at all, and that bothers me too.

There is a tree.

A tree so tall, it towers over me, and I have absolutely no idea how two short women managed to cover the entire thing in decorations and lights in the span of a day.

"Alexei!" Elena says, her joy oozing from her words. "Look what the new lady of the house has done!"

New lady of the house.

Magdalena's brown eyes turn on me, her cherry-red lips tilted in an expectant lilt.

"Do you like it?"

My heart slams in my chest.

I can't see the room. Not anymore. All that I see around me is my mother. The happiness she had when putting out the decorations. The way she used to hold me up to the tree to place the decorations.

The smell of her underneath the citrus-sweet smell that's dominating the air.

Grief.

That is what claws at my chest.

Grief. Loss. I feel the absence of my mother like a bullet wound. No, not a single bullet. A shotgun wound, a gaping hole in my chest that I can't seem to fill, and that can't be repaired by any number of stitches.

My ears ring, and the sounds of the festive music turn to a screech in my mind.

I miss her.

The thought bubbles forward, and it feels like it's going to break me.

I have not missed my mother in...

Years.

I have not allowed myself to miss her. I have not allowed myself to feel the grief that's ripping me apart. My blood sizzles through my veins, and my heart pounds against the edges of my ribs.

I have to get out of here.

I turn and run.

The hallways of Orlov House twist around me. The portraits of my ancestors seem to leer, ashamed of my cowardice.

Ashamed of the depth of loss that's drowning me right now.

My footsteps beat, a drum that matches the pounding in my chest. I run until I find myself in a room covered in draped sheets, ghosts that are illuminated only by the pale light coming from the large windows that look over the grounds.

Her rooms.

It's dark in here. Quiet. I hiss out a breath, trying to get myself under control.

I almost have it.

Then, I hear a sweet, resonant voice.

"Alexei?"

I screw my eyes shut. "Not now, Magdalena."

I wish she would take the hint.

"Alexei. Look. I'm sorry, I don't know…"

"That's right," I spin, snarling at her. "You don't know."

Magdalena freezes.

I come up on her. "You don't know, Magdalena! You have no idea! You don't know who I am! You don't know me! You have no idea what you've done! Those decorations, that room, this room…" I heave a breath in, the words disappearing on my tongue.

I'm yelling. I know I am.

But Magdalena stands strong in front of me.

"You have no idea what you've done," I finish.

She studies me. I can tell she's afraid; the paleness of her face reflects in the moonlight.

But she does not relent. And she does not back down.

Instead, she tips her chin and folds her arms and looks at me.

"You're right. Of course I don't know. Because you haven't told me, Alexei. I don't know what this room is. I don't know what the decorations mean to you. I don't know what the hell you want from me, other than to be the ticket to just have this empty, old house. You know, why do you even want this house if you're just going to let it rot?"

I seethe. "I will not let Orlov House rot."

"Oh yeah? Because the way you're going, if you keep it up, you're not going to fill it with a family."

I freeze.

She huffs. "I might be your wife but I'm not a broodmare. If you want to have children, you have to talk to me. Let me know why you hate the decorations. You have to be sweet. You have to seduce me," she says.

My mind hangs on that word.

"You think I could not seduce you?" I growl.

She rolls her eyes. "No, I don't—"

I do not let her finish that sentence.

My hands grip her face, and with a rough tug, I bring her face to mine.

The moment that my lips descend on hers, I know that my world is about to change.

And, that I have made a colossal mistake.

MAGGIE

❄

A lexei's lips on mine are...
Everything.

Somehow, in the span of seconds, my whole world is reduced to this.

His lips.

His mouth.

His hands on my face.

His tongue, slipping into my mouth, tangling with mine in a deep, consuming kiss.

I've never been kissed like this.

I mean I've definitely been kissed. But comparing those kisses to this one is like comparing rocks to... apples.

This is the type of kiss that makes me feel alive.

I moan, shrugging into his arms. He wraps a fist in my hair, tugging my head back to deepen the kiss.

Holy cow.

I gasp again as he breaks the kiss, his lips trailing down my neck. I moan as they trace against the sensitive place where my neck and shoulder meet, and gasp again as he pushes my silk button-down shirt off of my shoulder.

"You bought clothes," he growls under his breath.

"You told me to," I murmur.

That seems to make him very happy. He grunts, the noise sounding satisfied. "What else will you do if I tell you to, Magdalena?"

I shiver, because I'm kind of afraid to answer that question.

Alexei's fingers grasp, covering my breast. I moan as he kneads me through the light silk of my shirt.

His kiss is like fire.

I feel hot everywhere, despite the chill of the room. I can feel his kiss in every part of my body. I can feel it from the bottoms of my feet to the top of my head.

Alexei's kiss is like holding onto a live wire.

He makes my body light up like an electrical storm. I can't even hide the fact that I'm insanely aroused…

And, that I'm making out with him in the room that he yelled at me for being in before.

I back off, breaking the kiss.

Alexei and I have too much… stuff between us to be doing this here.

Too much that we don't know. Too much that's gone unsaid.

Too much that we need to figure out before we can be making out

Alexei's chest is heaving. He opens his eyes slowly. They're so blue, and they seem to glow as he looks at me.

For a second, I think he's going to say something.

Then, his face shutters, and he turns from me.

Shit.

Shit.

"Alexei…"

"That was a mistake," he growls.

I blink. "What?"

"I did not mean to do that."

"Oh," I whisper.

"It is just… it is the room. And the decorations."

And now we're right back where we started. "Tell me about the decorations, Alexei."

He pauses.

I shut my eyes and pull out the big guns. "Please."

I swear I can hear the snow falling outside.

Alexei takes a deep breath. "My mother… she loved to decorate for the holiday."

"Your mother?"

"She passed when I was a teenager," he whispers.

My eyes widen.

I wondered where all the decorations came from. Elena just pointed me to them and said that they belonged to the lady of the house…

Who I totally assumed meant me.

I shut my eyes. "And I dragged all of the decorations out, and it reminded you of your mom."

"This was her room," he murmurs.

Shoot.

"Alexei… I'm so sorry."

He's dead silent.

Opening my eyes, I look at where he's standing, so close to me, but so far away. "Sorry. I guess that I just got caught up in the moment. Sorry. I didn't mean to upset you. I just… I'm sorry," I whisper.

Alexei is quiet.

Finally, his head bobs and he looks down at me.

"You didn't know."

"But now I do. I can take them down…"

"No."

I freeze.

Alexei clears his throat. "No. They brought you and Elena joy, did they not?"

"Yes. My mom and I always decorate a lot for the holiday."

"Then keep them. Please," he murmurs. "I… I will return to Novgorod. I will stay there through the new year."

"Oh…"

"I do want you to be my wife, Magdalena. And I don't wish to treat you as a broodmare. I wish to have a… I wish to make sure it is not bad."

I snort. "Oh, I don't think it's going to be bad if that's how you kiss."

Oh.

Shit.

I clap my fingers over my mouth. "Oh my god. Pretend I didn't say that out loud."

Alexei's voice carries a tone of humor. "I will pretend."

"Thanks," I whisper.

The thought of spending Christmas alone… well. It sucks.

But I understand.

If the loss of his mother was so painful that he can't even look at Christmas decorations…

I get that.

He turns to go. Instinctively, I kind of reach for him.

It's not that I don't want him, or the future he's offering.

I do want it.

I want it very, very badly. I want to do more than just kiss him. I can't deny that I'm crazy attracted to him.

But my fingers curl around empty air.

"Alexei," I call.

He freezes.

"If you... if you wanted to stay. You could," I whisper.

He doesn't move.

"Being alone on Christmas would suck. For both of us," I add. "If we're going to be... if we're going to do this, maybe we should spend the time doing something else."

He turns, and the hungry look on his face makes my stomach clench.

"I mean. We could get to know each other. So that things like... the decorations... they don't happen again."

Alexei studies me.

"Perhaps," he murmurs.

Then, he's gone.

I give him a minute, then quietly, I close the door to his mother's room behind me.

I'm okay with giving Alexei space. If he needs it.

This might not be love.

But I think that if we both just... try, it could be something else.

Something that I'm okay with, even if it's not what I'm dreaming of.

ALEXEI

"Boss. The car is not going anywhere," Anatoly growls.

Looking outside at the blizzard, I have to agree.

It's early. I spent a restless night watching the snow slowly build; the kiss that I explored with Magdalena simmering through my veins.

I could not sleep.

Not when the memory of her lips on mine was so... present. Not when I could practically taste her still, sugar and mint, and when my body still thrummed with energy from caressing the delectable curves of her body.

My wife.

One of the very, very obvious advantages of having a wife is slowly becoming clear to me.

I do not need to try hard to find someone to have sex with. I am the head of the Orlov family. I am rich. I can find women wherever I want.

The problem is that I do not often want. I am a busy man, and I have spent much of my time building the empire that my father entrusted to me before his death.

Having a wife, or the process of obtaining one, was never part of my plan.

But now that I have one?

One that tastes so sweet, one whose body calls to mine in a siren song?

I find myself faced with the realization that I am not sure if I can keep my hands off of her. And since I will see her again, which is unusual for me when it comes to my trysts...

I am uncertain what to do.

Anatoly clears his throat as we stand in the main entrance to the house. The snow outside is truly something out of legend.

It's a storm that I also would not wish to travel in.

I glance at him. "Your family is in the village?"

He nods. Orlov House, and the estate around it, hosts a very small village. In the old days, the denizens were the serfs of our family.

Now, though, they're regular citizens.

As regular as a citizen can be in Russia, I suppose.

Still, I take the duty of protecting them quite seriously. I do ensure that they're not bullied by any local oligarchs, and that I attend all of the local festivals and events in my somewhat ceremonial role.

We have that, I suppose.

"Can you make it to the village?"

Anatoly snorts. "There is no blizzard that could keep me from my home, Boss."

I figured that was the case. Even if there is a blizzard that would keep him from taking me back to Novgorod.

To be fair, it is a much longer drive. But...

I decide not to press the issue.

With one final nod, Anatoly leaves.

I sigh and head back into the kitchen.

"So you'll be staying with us, then?" Elena says as she glides into the kitchen.

I can't help but note how smug she is about that.

"Yes. Until the storm lifts."

"Ah, well. The storm will lift whenever the storm lifts. Until then, we can enjoy some of your favorite foods, no?"

I arch an eyebrow. "And did you also happen to get all the food to celebrate the holiday with?"

Elena waves her hand at me. "Oh, you know. It is the lady's first time having Christmas in Russia. And the New Year. She hasn't even experienced the Russian New Year. I will make sure she knows how wonderful it is," she says with a smile.

My heart constricts, thinking of the holidays in front of me.

"It is okay to miss her, you know."

I look over at Elena.

"You did not get the chance to miss her. Not right away. Your father... he took you quickly to his side."

"He did what he needed to," I respond stiffly.

Elena nods. "And may he rest in peace. But now, your father is gone too. You have the chance to remember her, to miss her. You have the chance to experience a new life, with your wife."

I snort. "I don't need a new life, Elena. I like mine—"

"Perfectly well, I know. You don't need to remind me," she cuts me off. "But, darling, what if it was so much more than just perfectly well? What if you could have the peace that you once did?"

I glare at her. "I am at peace."

"You are many things. I have not seen you at peace in many years."

I growl. "Elena. I am who I am to protect the house and the family."

She nods. "Maybe. But your father has given you the skills to navigate that. You have to decide who you are. Are you your father's son? Or are you your mother's?"

For some reason, that hits me somewhere in my chest.

I don't respond.

Elena smiles. "I will make breakfast. The lady will be awake soon. She enjoys very sweet coffee, like all Americans."

"Why do I need to know this?" I grumble, eyeing the expensive espresso machine that I brought to the house in an effort to modernize it.

"In case you wish to have a cup ready for her," Elena winks.

She leaves the room.

I take a minute to stare at the machine, regarding the mugs next to it.

I don't know how long she will be sleeping for. The kitchen is the informal place to take breakfast.

But, I suppose that I would like a coffee as well.

She enjoys very sweet coffee.

Fuck it.

Let us see how sweet the little American girl can be.

❈

I have just finished making the latte when Magdalena walks in.

She freezes in the doorway, and I can tell in that moment that she is just as affected by the kiss as I was.

Or, that she's perplexed to see me here.

Mentally, I thank Elena for giving me the hint about coffee as a way to break the awkward silence.

I turn, offering it to her. "I heard you like very sweet coffee."

She flushes. It's a pretty expression that makes my eyes trace the blush down the smooth column of her throat, and fantasize about where it disappears into the soft cream of her sweater. "Elena keeps saying that, but I swear I just like a regular amount of sweetness."

"Americans tend to take their coffee sweeter than Russians."

"Well, if by that you mean that I don't like it strong enough to strip paint, then yeah," she murmurs.

I laugh.

I can't help it. Magdalena's quick wit is very much entertaining to me.

Her eyes round a little at my laughter, as though she's surprised by it.

My chest sinks. Does she really think me such a monster?

You're the bigger monster.

I shake off the thought. Offering the mug, I tilt my head. "Do you want it?"

After a moment, she nods. "Let me see what you're working with here." She takes the cup from my fingers, and I note that she's careful not to brush against me as she does so.

Is she repulsed by me?

Doubt cuts through me.

Still, I watch as she takes the cup and presses it to her lips. I have to look away as she drinks, because seeing her perfect plump lips makes my mind wander to other uses for them.

Or how they felt underneath mine as she yielded so sweetly to my kiss.

"Okay. You might have done something good here," she says, her voice throaty.

I train my gaze back on her.

Magdalena sips again, her eyes closing. "This is good."

"I aim to please."

I hadn't intended the statement to be quite so... enticing.

But the way her eyes snap open and meet mine, I fully see how she interpreted it that way.

My lips curl slightly in satisfaction.

"Well. I guess mission accomplished," she whispers.

Elena bustles into the kitchen then, and the tension breaks.

We both sit, and Elena provides a delicious breakfast of blini and preserved fruits. Elena and Magdalena chatter while we eat, and I can't help but consider how... domestic this is.

And with the snow, falling in sheets and hissing slightly against the windows?

It is just as Elena described.

Peaceful.

While I have not necessarily felt chaotic, or frantic, or any other word that stands opposite of this peaceful feeling, I do notice now how nice it is.

Elena gives me a knowing look toward the end of the meal. "Maggie, dochka, have you ever experienced a Russian holiday before?"

I want to roll my eyes at the endearment. *Dochka. Doll.*

She is a doll. As pretty as one, anyway.

Magdalena shakes her head. "No. I assume it's pretty different from an American Christmas?"

Elena clicks her tongue. "Oh, most certainly. What would you do for an American Christmas?"

Magdalena sighs. "Nothing huge. We'd decorate, listen to music. Bake cookies. Decorate them. Play in the snow if it snowed. Look at Christmas lights. Read books by the fire."

"We do all of those. Except perhaps the cookies," Elena smiles. "Maybe you could show us what those are?"

Magdalena perks up. "I'd love to."

"And Alexei, perhaps you could tell Maggie about some of the ornaments on the tree?"

I raise an eyebrow.

Elena shrugs. "Just an idea. They are family heirlooms, after all. She should know the history of the family if she is to be the lady of the house."

"It's okay, I don't want to intrude—"

"Come," I say, rising. "I will tell you about them."

I can see Magdalena startle, as though she wasn't expecting me to be so forthcoming. I myself am not expecting it.

But Elena has a point.

Maybe it is the peace. Maybe it is the consistent thrum of the snow against the windows.

But for some reason, the memories that I keep tightly locked under my skin feel a little looser today. The ache in my chest does not feel quite so painful.

Instead, it feels...

Manageable.

Magdalena stands cautiously.

I reach my hand forward, and the wait for her to take it feels like an eternity.

When she does, I can't help the shiver that courses through me.

"Let us see the tree," I murmur.

MAGGIE

❄

I feel like I'm torn between the reality of waking up and looking at Alexei today, and the memory of the kiss last night.

Well.

Maybe it's better to say that I'm *haunted* by last night's kiss.

I didn't sleep. Not even a little. The room was super cozy and warm, even with the storm howling outside, but I couldn't sleep while I was so keyed up over that kiss.

Keyed up is an understatement. On fire is probably more accurate.

I've never been so turned on by a kiss. Not ever.

And given the emotional turmoil of the night, I'm not really sure what to do with that.

So when I found Alexei sitting in the kitchen, a coffee made for me in hand, I approached the situation like I'd approach a wild bear.

Cautiously.

Knowing that I probably shouldn't, but that I was going to anyway.

The coffee was good, though. And then Elena suggested that Alexei show me the ornaments on the tree. And then I said no because I wanted him to have an easy out that didn't involve making Elena sad.

And then he invited me to do it anyway.

I'm not sure that I can hang in here with all of these emotional ups and downs.

I'm not really used to things being this chaotic. For the most part, my childhood has been steady and calm. Until the house fire, the scariest thing that ever happened to me was being picked on by Heather Mastronardi for having purple hair when I was in seventh grade.

Well. And some teasing about my weight, but I'm pretty sure every teenage girl has been through that.

I'm just not really equipped for this roller coaster.

At least, that's what I tell myself as I follow Alexei into the large room with the Christmas tree.

There's a roaring fire, which infuses the room with warmth that feels so good, I want to flop onto the comfortable furniture and curl up with a good book. Between that and the snow swirling against the windows, the room is unbearably cozy, and I can't believe how nice it is in here.

Alexei must notice my reaction. He turns to me. "You did a good job with the decorations."

I stiffen up. "Yes. Sorry. I know that it's hard because of your mom—"

"Which you couldn't have known about unless Elena or I told you. She didn't, and I should have," he says.

Huh.

Alexei takes another step toward me. He's wearing what I assume is the Alexei version of casual clothes; dress pants and a black button-down shirt. The fabric is kind of silky, and seems to slip over his hard body, caressing his muscles in a way that's downright indecent.

I gulp at the memory of exactly how much strength is contained there.

Because now that I know?

I can never forget.

"Magdalena?"

"Maggie," I say automatically.

Then, realizing that he was trying to snap me out of my zone out, I freeze.

I'm definitely staring at him.

Alexei's lips tilt up in a smile. "What were you thinking about, just now?"

"Nothing," I say quickly.

Maybe a little too quickly.

"Nothing at all?"

"No," I gulp.

He steps closer.

"I think you might be lying, Magdalena."

I snort. "You don't know me well enough to know that."

"Oh. I think I do very much know you well enough."

"No," I shake my head. "You don't."

"You weren't thinking, perhaps, of a kiss just now?"

I freeze.

Alexei's probably six inches away from me.

He leans forward, and if I tipped my face up, then our lips would be right there...

"Magdalena?"

"N...No..." I whisper. "I wasn't."

He makes a low, humming noise.

"Pity."

"Why?" I ask.

"I was thinking about it."

My jaw literally drops open.

Alexei's eyes sparkle. "You didn't think that I would be affected by kissing you, did you?"

"I... uh... no?"

He inhales sharply.

"Let us say this. Since so far we have only told each other the truth, I will not stop now. The truth, Magdalena, is that I have never wanted a wife... until I realized how very entertaining it would be to have one."

"Entertaining?"

"Kissing you, Magdalena, reminded me of the very strong benefits of having a wife. "

"Like what?" I whisper.

I don't know why I'm asking. It's like I'm drawn to him, drawn to the things he's saying.

Since we've so far only told each other the truth.

"The benefits of the way you taste. The feel of your skin under mine. The way I want you to scream my name," he practically purrs.

I gulp. "Um. You don't have to have a wife for that," I say breathlessly.

Alexi's grin is hungry and dark.

"And yet, I find myself drawn to my wife... just for that."

His hands are slowly skating up my arms now. I shiver at the warmth radiating from them.

"I won't take other lovers, Magdalena. In case you were worried about that."

"I... okay," I whisper. I wasn't exactly worried about it, but I guess it's good to know anyway.

"And I expect the same from you."

I bark out a laugh. "Who could I possibly do that with?"

"No one," he growls, his blue eyes darkening. "Because you're mine."

My head tips up, some kind of sassy response on my lips...

But it dies.

Quickly.

Because Alexei's lips on mine end any thoughts in my mind.

I explode.

There's no other word for it. His hands are everywhere. His mouth on mine makes me ache, and when his tongue laps at me, begging me to open for him. I do.

I've never felt anything like this.

The smell of citrus and spice in the air is intense, and mixed with Alexei's dark scent I feel lightheaded.

Or, that could be the fact that his hands are tugging on my skirt.

Alexei's hands come to my hips, and I squeak when he leans me down onto the comfortable couch. With a motion, he pulls me on top of him...

Then I moan, arching my back, as I realize that I can sense how much he wants me. It feels like another gem of truth, one that I'm holding onto with both hands.

Namely, the way his body is reacting, which sends me into a sort of frenzy.

I need more of him.

Rocking over the hardness that's between his legs, I gasp when Alexei's lips touch my neck.

"I compliment you on your taste," he grunts when his fingers tease at the edge of the soft cashmere on my shoulder, "but please, please take this off."

I comply.

The sweater comes up, drifting like gossamer over my head, until I'm bare from the waist up.

Except for the equally as expensive lingerie that I treated myself to.

I thought that the lingerie might have been a little bit of a splurge. I haven't exactly treated myself to something so pretty in... well. Ever, I guess.

I thought it was pretty. I think I look good in it.

However, I don't know if that's just me.

So when Alexei sees my breasts, framed in fabric that costs more than a semester of my tuition, I'm a little insecure...

Until his rough hands palm them and I moan, arching into his touch.

"You're so fucking pretty, Magdalena," he rasps before he laps at one of my nipples, pulling down the expensive lace to reveal my breast to him.

I gasp.

I'm not used to men worshiping my body. I've always been too curvy, too much.

But Alexei touches me like he can't get enough.

"Magdalena," Alexei says roughly from where he's kissing my chest. "I need more of you. I want more..."

"Don't stop," I whisper.

He looks up at me. "Magdalena..."

"Don't stop. Please," I beg.

Alexei growls again.

I squeak when he flips me onto the couch, my back against the soft surface. My skirt comes off, sliding down and off of my hips onto the floor.

Propping myself up on my elbows, I look down at Alexei.

He's staring up at me, kneeling on the ground.

I open my mouth. Close it.

The way his eyes flash looks dangerous.

Slowly, he takes my knees and pushes them apart. I wince.

He pauses. "Are you hurt?"

"No," I whisper.

"Then what is the problem?"

I look to the side. "Um... no one has ever.. I mean you don't have to..." I don't know how to tell him that normally, the thickness of my thighs isn't something that people exactly like.

"Magdalena," he rumbles.

I look down.

"You are so fucking beautiful. Do you not see how much I want you?" he murmurs.

I mean, I can. His thin grey pants hide very little when it comes to that.

His fingers skate up, wrapping in the sides of my very expensive panties.

"If no one has done this before, then I would be more than happy to show you. And to make sure no one will ever have this from you again," he growls.

I raise my eyebrows.

"You're mine. My wife. Mine," he practically snarls.

"Alexei. I'm yours," I whisper.

The affirmation seems to calm him slightly.

"I want to make you come, Magdalena," Alexei looks at me, his eyes caressing down my legs. "I want to taste you."

I've never had anyone *want* to do that before.

So, despite my heart slamming against my ribs, I nod.

I open my legs.

And Alexei grins. He kneels on the floor, and I quickly adjust, worried that his knees are going to hurt.

Alexei watches, then looks up at me with eyes glittering with interest. "You're worried for me?"

"Well yeah, you're kneeling on the hard floor," I protest.

He chuckles.

"I only kneel for one person, Magdalena. And that is my wife."

I would say something but...

All thoughts fly out of my mind when he hooks my legs over his shoulders.

When he licks me at the center of the heat that's driving me crazy, I arch off of the couch.

"Fuck, Magdalena," he growls. "You taste like... fuck," he grunts.

I would say something, because it feels like I should.

But I can't.

All I can do is feel.

Every inch of my skin tingles. I can feel the sensation of his tongue the whole way through my body, practically sizzling through my skin.

I want this to never, ever end.

Alexei's tongue is incredible. His mouth laps and nips and sucks in all the right places. At some point I drag my fingers through his hair, pushing him down, because he's just right *there...*

He pulls back, licking his lips. "What do you think of this now?" he asks.

"Yes," I breathe.

He laughs.

Alexei's breath on my center makes me arch up against him.

"What do you need from me, love?" He whispers.

Love.

The word feels... soon. Too soon.

But I can't pretend it doesn't feel good.

His tongue laps at me again, and I hook my legs over his shoulders, tugging him toward me.

"Oh," he chuckles, the laugh clearly radiating over my heated core. "You do like this, don't you?"

"Sorry," I gasp. For a second, I'm flooded with doubt. Is that not okay? Should I not like it this much?

I pull my legs back, but Alexei's big hands grasp them, pulling them firmly down towards him.

"I love it, Magdalena. Take what you need," he murmurs.

I gulp. "I... I've never... I've never done this..."

What he doesn't know is that I haven't done *any* of this.

I haven't dated a lot. Really. I haven't. and I haven't had sex.

At all.

Ever.

His eyes seem to glow. "Are you a virgin for me, Magdalena?"

I nod.

The noise he makes is positively feral.

"Have you ever touched yourself before?"

I nod.

"Good. What makes you come when you do?"

I wriggle again. "Um. Well. I've never really... not without... help," I finish lamely.

I swear the blood drains out of his face. "Do you use toys when you make yourself come?"

God, his voice. It's like an extra set of hands, rasping over my skin. I moan, my eyes fluttering as I writhe against him.

"Answer me, wife," he snaps.

"Yes, okay," I whisper. "I do. I have a vibrator and..."

"Did you bring it with you?"

"No," I whisper.

He murmurs.

Then, I feel one thick finger press inside me.

I moan.

Alexei cusses in Russian. "You're so wet for me, darling."

"Yes. Please. I…"

"I know what you need," he grunts.

Then, his lips move in combination with his fingers.

And I can barely hang on.

My skin feels like it's too tight. Sensations chase over my body, each one more amplified than the next.

When he adds another finger, I practically shudder around him.

When his lips tug on my clit, sucking, I scream.

"Come for me, love," he whispers.

I don't know if it's the endearment or the motion, but my orgasm crashes over me, taking me completely by surprise.

It's the most extreme feeling I've ever had.

Like, I'm pretty sure that I can see stars. Or heaven.

Or both.

I'm vaguely aware of Alexei removing his fingers, the sound kind of obscene. The loss of heat from him moving away from me makes me shiver.

Alexei moves up, his big body arching over mine, his arms on either side of my head. I'm panting, staring at him, and he stares down at me.

Oh no. Does he want me to…

Gently, he presses a kiss to my head.

"We never looked at the ornaments," he murmurs.

I laugh.

I can't help it. I'm lying on the couch, mostly naked, and Alexei is fully clothed. Any of the staff could walk in at any time.

And I think I might have just screamed.

"Are the ornaments really the highest priority at the moment?" I murmur into the cool air.

Alexei drapes a blanket over me. "If you want them to be, then they will be."

I rise up, my hands coming up to hold the blanket over myself. It's so soft, and I let my fingers dance over it.

Alexei's eyes trace the movement.

I'm not sure what to do right now. I kind of want more. I want to know what he's like. What having a husband is like, in every sense of the word.

But I'm also scared.

Alexei is so hot and cold. One second he's telling me I'm beautiful, the next he's telling me to get out. He hands me a coffee, and drags me to look at the ornaments he said he never wanted to see.

I don't know him.

Loneliness punches through me and I pull back slightly.

Alexei's face twists. He pulls his hand back.

Now, I feel bad.

"Alexei..."

"What did you say that your holiday tradition was? Making cookies?"

I nod.

He takes a breath. "Then, I think we should do that next."

Alexei turns to gather my clothes, but I can't help the question that punches out of me.

"Why?"

He looks back at me.

We have always been honest. Don't stop now. Please.

"Because, Magdalena. I find myself curious about my new wife. I want to know what I stole you away from, and how I might make it up to you. I know this is not the holiday you wished for. I would at least like to try," he says softly.

I blink. "Really?"

"If you are asking me of my honesty… yes. We do not lie to each other," he murmurs.

I don't know how this whole truth thing came to be part of our very, very new marriage but…

I trust it.

More than that, I really like it.

Both of those things help solidify my decision for me.

Nodding, I take my sweater from him.

"Let me change, and I'll meet you in the kitchen."

❄

After a quick internet search converting metric to US measuring units, and lots of help from Elena, I'm fully ready to make sugar cookies.

I'm mixing them together when I feel a warm presence at my back.

"Alexei," I breathe.

"Hmm," he murmurs. His lips touch my neck and I shiver.

The kiss he places is fast. Just a brush of his lips against me.

But the tenderness there is downright domestic.

It makes me ache.

"So. Tell me of these... cookies."

I raise my eyebrow. "You don't make cookies in Russia?"

"We make a variety of treats," Alexei shrugs. "I think American cookies are probably different."

"Well, first, tell me. Did you make anything like these with your mom?"

He shakes his head. "In Russia, we spend more time on New Year's than Christmas. I think the old holiday ways are still dominant in Novgorod and nearby, but the fact that we were a country without religion for so long changed a lot of the holidays."

"That doesn't answer my question, and kind of sounds like a bad joke."

"A joke?" he tilts his head.

I nod. "You know. The old 'in Russia, you don't have holidays. Holidays have *you*," I emphasize with a fake Russian accent.

Alexei's face is completely neutral. "I have never heard this. And I don't sound like that."

"I don't sound like that," I mimic in my fake accent.

I'm teasing him.

The thought strikes me like a lightning bolt. I'm sitting here *teasing* Alexei, like we're...

Like we're a real married couple.

A real smile crosses his lips. "You like my accent, Magdalena?"

"Maggie," I roll my eyes. "Seriously, I think... at this point, call me Maggie."

"At this point?" he repeats softly.

I glance over from where I'm wrapping the cookie dough to chill.

Alexei's eyes are burning into mine. "You said your friends and family call you Maggie."

"I did," I whisper, nibbling at my bottom lip.

His eyes catch the gesture and darken further, his face taking on a hungry look.

I stop.

Alexei glances up at me. "You count me among your friends or family?"

"Well, you are my husband. And you've seen me naked. So I think you're kind of well on the way," I murmur.

He looks at me.

"Maggie," he murmurs.

In his accent, the word seems to creep over my skin. I shiver, and he moves closer.

"Are you cold?" he whispers.

"No."

"Then why..."

I pull out of his arms. "Anyway. Um. We need to put these in the fridge and then we'll roll them out later. And decorate them," I say quickly, putting the dough to chill.

When I close the door, he's frowning. "A great deal of steps before they're done."

I shrug. "Yeah well. Good things take time."

I meant it about the cookies. But, Alexei seems to deflate a little.

Oh no. I didn't mean to imply anything about him, or our marriage. Trying to salvage the moment, I smile. "Don't tell me that you're like... such a badass that you've never made cookies before."

"I have had treats prepared for me before," he murmurs.

I flush.

"Well. We just need to wait a while."

"And what will we do while we wait?" he murmurs.

Okay. There's *definitely* some lust in his tone.

Alexei catches my wrist and tugs me close. I curl into his arms, ready for a kiss.

He surprises me by hugging me.

It's a nice hug. I'm stiff for a second, just because I don't expect it, but after a minute I melt into his embrace.

We stand there in the kitchen for so long, it's beginning to get kind of weird.

I'm the one who pulls back first. "That was nice," I say softly.

Alexei puts his hand on my cheek. "I am not nice."

"Okay. But it was a nice hug."

His thumb moves over my face.

"I'm sorry, Maggie," he says abruptly.

I open my eyes. "Why?"

"You didn't ask for this. For me."

My eyes pop open, and I study him.

Alexei is looking at me with... something that looks like sadness. Sincerity.

It tugs at my chest.

I sigh. "Look. We're honest with each other. That's what we're doing. Right?"

"Yes," he says softly. "I would like that."

I nod. "Good. You're right. I didn't ask for this. But there are lots of things in life people don't ask for. I wanted to go to school and be a therapist. I wanted to help people. I might still be able to do that, someday, but this came up, and I'm fine with it. Life throws things at you, Alexei. You can either fight them or roll with the punches, and as long as you're not awful to me, I'm fine here. My mom is safe. I'm safe. For now, that's all I need. If you want to give me more, if you want to actually build a life together, then I could do that. But for now, we're married. I'm safe. My mom is safe. And I'm pretty content to live with it."

His lips tug into a small frown. "But you would not have chosen me."

"No," I say honestly.

Alexei seems to shrink.

God. Whatever his dad did to him... "But I would like to."

He glances at me.

I take Alexei's hand and pull him close. "We're stuck together. We could make that go a lot of ways. But if you want, Alexei, I could still choose you. To be with you. To…"

I stop.

I can't promise to love him. Because if I promise it, then it isn't really a choice.

Keeping my promises is important to me. I won't make a promise I can't keep.

"What does that mean, Maggie?"

"Let's get to know each other. Let's take some time to choose each other," I whisper.

He looks at where our hands are joined. "But we are already married."

"And? We can't… date?"

He chuckles. "Date? We are stuck in a Russian mansion. I do not know when the snow will give up."

"Then I guess we better get creative," I wink.

Alexei's eyes sparkle.

"I've got the first date planned already," I announce.

"Oh?"

"Yes. In about two hours, get ready, because you're going to decorate these cookies," I wink.

Alexei's lips tuck into a grin. "And after?"

"I guess we better see how good you are at planning an indoor date."

ALEXEI

❄

It is a busy two hours.

But, by the end of it, I believe I have a plan to date my own wife.

While snowed in.

During the lead up to a time of year that I've done my very, very best to forget completely.

When I come back to the kitchen, Maggie (the name still feels strange in my mind) has sheets of cookie dough rolled out. She's using a knife to cut shapes out of the dough.

There's a spot of flour on her hip, and I want to run my hands over it...

So I do.

Maggie releases the most delightful little squeak. I grin, looking down at her.

"You scared me!"

"You never have to be scared when you're around me," I whisper into her hair.

She flushes that pretty shade of red, and I move to the side.

"Maggie," I murmur, noticing her smile at the name. "What is this?"

"Well apparently cookie cutters aren't a thing in this kitchen so.. I'm making do."

"Cookie cutters?"

She nods. "Yeah. You're supposed to make the dough into shapes. Then we'll put icing on them."

I study the scene in front me, then plant a kiss on her cheek. "Hold on," I murmur.

Quickly, I dash from the room, returning moments later with some thick pieces of wire.

"What shape do you wish for?"

Maggie arches an eyebrow. "Oh, usually it's like... stars, circles, mittens. Candy canes. Bells."

"Bells?" I tilt my head.

"You know. The bells of Christmas?"

I shake my head. "Bells it is."

Using my hands, and occasionally things in the kitchen, I bend the lengths of wire into approximations of the shapes she requires.

"These are pretty good," Maggie says, picking one up.

"Even if you can't press them into the dough, you could trace around them," I say.

She smiles. "That's downright impressive, Alexei."

Her praise makes me feel warmer than any fire.

We settle in to work together. The oven behind us hums, and the silence feels...

Companionable.

Is this what it is to have a wife? Companionship?

I'm not sure if it's the season, or if it's merely the room, but I feel...

Content.

Maggie walks me through the process of placing the cookies in the oven. By the time they're done, a new tray is ready to bake, and so on until all of the dough has been baked into the small shapes.

Maggie produces sweet white frosting, and we proceed to decorate.

I look at where she's trying to paint a face on a star. "A face?"

"Yes. My mom always put faces on them. Said it made them look happier for the season."

"I don't see how a face will do that."

She rolls her eyes. "Well, it doesn't matter. When I was a kid I just wanted to lick the frosting off anyway, so I think she probably said that just to make sure I had something to do so I didn't eat all of the frosting."

Lick the frosting...

An idea forms in my mind. I take my spoon, pull some of the sticky liquid...

And dollop it on her face.

Maggie's jaw drops. "Alexei! What..."

Quickly, I swoop in, and lick the frosting off of her.

Her face goes that delightful, perfect shades of crimson.

My cock is throbbing now. I lean in and press a kiss on her lips.

"Perhaps I can tempt you to lick the frosting after all?"

Her pupils go wide with lust.

A hungry growl forms in my throat. Quickly, I sweep my hand across the large butcher block in the kitchen that we use for the preparation of food, knocking cookies everywhere as I go.

"Alexei..." she pauses.

I freeze. "They are beautiful. I will make one hundred more of them. But if I do not taste you right now, I will lose my mind," I growl at her.

Maggie's eyes widen, and when I lean down to pull her up and place her on the counter, she doesn't protest.

"Clothes," I grunt, tugging at her leggings.

She's halfway to doing as I ask when her eyes take on a devious gleam.

"What if I want to taste you?" she whispers.

Fuck.

Fuck.

She takes advantage of the way my body has completely frozen by sliding off of the counter and taking one of the bowls of icing.

Then, she kneels before me.

I'm a monster. I really am. Because the sight of her on her knees, her face level with my aching cock?

It's making me go insane.

"Alexei?" she asks.

Her beautiful brown eyes blink up at me, and it takes my brain a solid minute before I respond.

"You want to suck my cock, Maggie?" I say.

My voice is so hoarse with need, I barely recognize it.

She nods, her brown curls bouncing, and I have no choice but to continue.

"Take it out," I grunt.

She gently sets the pot of icing down, and then opens my belt. Her hands shake as they pull down my zipper, and I want to reassure her that...

What?

That she's perfect? that no matter what, she's already given me the best gift that I could have had?

"You're so fucking pretty, Maggie," I grunt. If she needs me to talk her through this, then I will certainly do so.

Her cheeks flush, but her hands stop shaking.

"So fucking pretty on your knees for me."

"I've never done this before," she whispers.

I swear, the words coming out in Russian because I don't know how to express these desires in English.

"What do I...."

"Take me in your hand," I grunt.

Her delicate fingers, still a little papery from the flour, curl around my cock.

My eyes roll back in my head and I sway.

"Alexei? Is that..."

"It's perfect," I moan. "Fuck, Maggie. Your hands feel so good. I could come from this alone."

"Oh," she murmurs.

"But if you put me between your lips..."

One of her hands disappears from my length, dipping into the pot of icing. The sensation of the cool icing dripping onto my cock, the fact that it's also white, much like another substance leaking from me...

"Fuck," I grunt.

Maggie looks up at me, smearing the sugar into the pre-cum leaking from the tip of me. "Like this?" she whispers.

Her tongue darts out, pink and wet, and laps at the sugar covering me.

The words pouring from me, in English and Russian, don't make sense. She runs her tongue over me, lapping up the mixture of my fluids and the sticky sugar.

"Maggie," I moan. "That's so good. You're so fucking sexy."

"Good," she whispers.

Good.

I growl. I want her to be good. I want this to be good. The teasing is killing me; however, it's time to move this along. "Be a good girl, and suck me."

Maggie obeys.

Her quick compliance is so fucking sexy. I watch her cheeks hollow as she takes me into her mouth, the strain clear on her face.

"You're doing so well, Maggie," I croon, one of my hands coming to pet her hair. "You take me so well. Go slow, darling. Take what you can."

Some kind of determination glints in her eyes, and she takes me deeper.

Fuck.

"I'm going to move, Maggie," I whisper. The urge to pump myself into her throat is too strong. "If it's too much, just lean back, okay?"

Her eyes look up at me, and the image of Maggie, her lips spread wide around my cock, a smear of white icing on her cheek, will be burned into my mind forever.

Slowly, gently, I pump my hips into her. I move back and forth, the motion slow and deliberate. I'm careful to not give her more than she can handle, but she surprises me by taking more and more with each thrust.

Finally, the orgasm builds at the edges of my spine. I grunt, pulling out.

Maggie's eyes widen. "Did I do it wrong?"

"No," I grit as I hold myself. "I'm going to come, and I don't…"

"I want to," she whispers.

I blink.

With delicacy, Maggie feeds me back into her mouth. I'm in awe. "Are you sure, Maggie?"

She nods.

Fuck.

I'm not going to last.

It takes only a few thrusts, and I can't hold back.

"Maggie," I pant. "I'm going to…"

She pulls me closer, and when I come, it is down her beautiful throat.

Maggie drinks me down, and when I finally pull from her sweet lips, I know that I'm never going to forget this.

More than that, I have a new mission.

I will win over my wife.

Because I will want this every day.

For the rest of my life.

MAGGIE

❄

The cookie making was my idea.

Sledding, apparently, is Alexei's.

I spent a restless night in my room, remembering all of the kisses. And, of course, the feeling of his cock in my mouth. And the fact that Alexei, in general, seems kind of...

Okay well, not "kind of".

A lot nicer than I thought he was.

Plus, I love that he's kind of agreed to do the whole 'date' thing. I mean clearly, right? Otherwise he wouldn't have participated in the cookies yesterday, or set up the sledding today. He's wrapped me in about a hundred layers of wool and down. I can barely move, and I'm pretty sure it's overkill.

That is, until we're actually outdoors.

"Holy crap," I whisper, my breath fogging as soon as it leaves my body. "It's cold out here."

Alexei laughs. "Why do you think winter is Russia's greatest war tactic?"

"I have no idea what that means. And my brain is frozen, so I can't even start," I say through clenched teeth.

Alexei turns around. "We can go back. As soon as you're ready, we can…"

"No," I interrupt him. "You want to sled? We sled. Let's do this."

I refuse to back down, even if I'm pretty sure I've never been closer to reenacting a Jack London novel.

Alexei chuckles and tugs the long wooden platform along. "Come. We will do a couple of runs and then go warm up."

"Warm up sounds nice," I mutter.

"You will be very pleased with the sauna then."

That does, in fact, sound pretty darn incredible.

Alexei marches us up to the top of a medium-sized hill. He settles himself on the sled, his long legs planting on either side of it as he anchors it into the snow.

He pats the space in front of him. "Come."

"I'm not sure I can fit there normally. Let alone as the Stay-Puft Marshmallow woman."

Alexei's eyebrow quirks. In the cold, his cheeks are rosy and his eyes shine.

He looks younger. Much less reserved.

A thought crosses my mind. "How old are you?"

"Thirty-five."

I whistle. "Dang. You're old."

Alexei laughs, and the sound is oddly muted in the cold. "That was abrupt."

"I'm only twenty-three," I smirk at him.

Alexei's eyes go hard. "Then I will look forward to showing you the ways of the world, milaya."

I roll my eyes, but the insinuation sends a chill down my spine. "Whatever, old man."

"Let's hear you say that after we go down this hill," Alexei laughs.

I do my best to settle myself onto the sled, and Alexei's body traps me in. He leans forward and presses a kiss on my cheek.

Through the burning cold, I feel it, and it makes my chest feel a little warmer.

"Are you ready?"

"I guess," I lean back into him.

I haven't been sledding since I was little. So little, in fact, that I don't remember going sledding at all, really.

I have no way to judge what's going to come next.

Alexei's strong legs push, and before I know it...

We're flying.

❄

"Okay. I have to admit. That was fun, but this is better," I sigh as I lean into the warmth of the sauna.

Alexei chuckles, the sound very, very close in the dark sauna.

After the sledding, which was admittedly pretty fun, Alexei brought me to one of the lower floors of the manor house. He instructed me to strip, handed me a towel, and then disappeared.

I did all of those things, and when I entered the large space, Alexei had already heated it up for us.

I lean back, inhaling the salt and moisture and the slightly herbal scent of the eucalyptus leaves. Alexei is next to me, and his big body stretches over multiple benches as he reclines.

He has a towel around his waist, but I still have a pretty stellar view, and I don't even hold back as I eye the sculpted lines of his abs.

"You're staring, milaya."

"What does that mean?" I ask, trying to deflect. I'm not going to admit that I am, in fact, staring at his amazing torso, but he doesn't need to know that.

Alexei cracks an eye, catching me.

I still don't look away.

"It is an endearment. Sweetheart. Dear. Darling," he purrs.

My skin prickles with awareness. "You moved to that pretty quickly."

"Did I?"

"Less than a week ago, you wouldn't even call me Maggie."

"Less than a week ago, I did not mean it," he murmurs.

That catches my attention.

Alexei shifts forward, all of those beautiful muscles flexing at once as he does. He puts his hands on his knees, and I'm mesmerized by the flex of his biceps as he runs his hands through his hair.

He's so beautiful.

I bet he makes beautiful babies.

The thought hits me like a ton of bricks… and is a great reminder that since I haven't been sexually active before, I'm not on any form of birth control.

The thought, however, fills me with a kind of bubbly interest that doesn't feel as terrifying as it has in the past.

I don't know that babies have ever crossed my mind. I don't know that I've ever really seen it as an option. Now that it is, though….

I'm kind of interested.

"I will always tell you the truth, milaya," he murmurs.

"So will I," I promise.

Alexei nods. "Good."

The silence in the sauna isn't scary. It actually feels… comforting.

I'm halfway asleep when Alexei sighs.

"I have enjoyed this day."

"Me too," I murmur.

He shifts. We're both sweaty, but I don't mind when he moves closer. I want to lick the moisture from his firm pecs, but I'm also kind of… too relaxed.

It's nice.

His lips graze the top of my head.

"I have one more surprise for you."

I straighten. Given the fact that we're still pretty naked, I was kind of thinking that we could pick up from where we left off the day before, in terms of exploring our... physical connection.

I tilt my head.

Alexi's grin is infectious.

"I will come collect you from your room."

❄

When Alexei grabs me from my room, he also does so with another surprise.

A silk scarf that he quickly wraps around my face as a blindfold.

I giggle, mostly to hide the way my skin shivers and my breath catches at his touch.

"Are you ready for your surprise?"

"Sure. I mean. It's a little unfair because ... this is your house. You can surprise me with anything."

"And yet, somehow you still continue to surprise me, milaya," he whispers.

I shiver again.

Alexei gently tugs on my hand, and I follow him.

"I swear, Alexei, this house is just not that big from the outside," I murmur as he guides me down yet another hallway. "There's simply no way that all of these halls exist."

"Maybe Orlov House is magical. Maybe it exists in multiple places at once," he whispers.

I laugh. "You're trying to pitch me on your magical house now too?"

"If it convinces you to love the house, yes."

My heart skips a little, because I don't think he meant *only* the house.

"I like Orlov House," I whisper.

I like you.

It's a surprising thought. I didn't think that I would be here so soon but...

I think I'm falling for Alexei.

Rationally, I know it's not possible. I haven't known Alexei long enough to fall for him. Things like love, actual, meaningful love, take time. Anything prior to really knowing him is just a chemical reaction. Just attraction.

But living it is an entirely different thing than recognizing it in a textbook.

I feel the same way around him as I feel around my mom. I mean... different, of course. I'm not sexually attracted to my mom.

But my heart is easy. I feel relaxed, and welcomed.

Seen.

All of these are things that I experience with love.

But you can't love him yet.

I keep that in my mind, because it's true. Attraction is instant.

Love takes time.

"Okay. We're here," he murmurs behind me.

My breath catches again as he tugs at the silk, and the feeling of it sliding off my face seems borderline indecent.

For a second, I blink. The light is still muted due to the continued storm, but it's bright enough that it takes me a minute to focus on the world around me.

And when I figure out what I'm looking at, I can't help it.

I gasp.

I'm in an enormous room. There are huge windows, floor-to-ceiling just like in Alexei's mom's room, but the furniture in this room isn't covered. Big, lush couches, huge long tables, and a fireplace that I could easily walk into dominate my view.

But beyond that?

Books.

Shelves and shelves of them, bordering the windows and lining the walls, stretching as far as I can see.

"Alexei..."

"Come in," he says, tugging my hand.

I can't do anything but follow.

He brings me over to an elegant desk carved out of blonde wood. My mouth drops as I see the shiny laptop, leather-bound notebook, and expensive pen set sitting there.

"What's this?"

"You were going to school. To be the... head doctor," he stumbles.

I smile. "Psychologist."

"Yes. Well. I do not know exactly, but I think you can finish your courses… here. Or you can find a new study. Russia has many fine learning institutions," he says.

I turn.

Alexei's eyes search mine.

My lips curl. "Alexei. Are you… rambling?"

He shakes his head like a dog shaking off water. "No. I do not ramble."

Huh. He's totally rambling.

Alexei Orlov is… nervous.

And I think I'm the only one who can make him feel better.

I walk forward. Leaning up on my tiptoes, I wrap my hands behind his neck.

He goes very, very still.

So still that, unless he leans down, I can't actually kiss him.

"Alexei," I murmur, tugging on his neck. "Let me kiss you."

He hesitates for just a second.

Just a tiny, tiny second.

Then, he leans down, and our lips meet.

Everything changes.

He kisses me like I'm the only fucking woman on earth, and I moan as I kiss him back.

My hands don't know what to grab. They roam over Alexei's neck and shoulders. I caress his broad back; I tug at his hair.

He groans and cups my face with one hand, the other one fisting in the base of my hair as he tips my head back to deepen our kiss. My clothes are too tight on me, and I wriggle as my sensitive skin demands to be exposed to his hands.

He pulls back and paints kisses down my neck. My eyes roll back in my head at the sensation. "Alexei," I pant, arching into his touch, "more."

"Whatever you want, I'll give it to you," he purrs.

I have a feeling that he doesn't just mean right now.

His hands find the edges of the comfortable shirt and pants that I've been wearing. We both struggle to get the last remnants of the sleeves off of my arms, as neither one of us is willing to break the heated kiss that we're sharing, but eventually I feel the cool air on the top of my breasts.

Alexei pulls back and rubs his hand over his mouth, staring at where I'm exposed to him. He swears in Russian.

"Maggie," he breathes. "When did you find such... alluring things to wear?"

I glance down at the expensive bra, then back up at him. "Well, I did some shopping. As it turns out, you get really good delivery service in Russia," I answer honestly. I bought this set, along with all the others, when I was mad at him and using his credit card like it was going out of style.

Little did I know that it would be him who seduced me, and how powerless I'd be to stop it.

"You will buy more," he growls as he looks at me.

I lean back onto the desk. Alexei carefully takes the computer and the writing items, tucking them out of the way.

Powerless.

That's how I feel. But not in a bad way.

In the best possible way.

However, I can still take back a little power. I lean back on my elbows, my skin meeting the hard surface of the deck. The motion presses my breasts up against the very expensive fabric. "If you like these, then I can definitely buy more," I purr.

"Maggie," his voice is hoarse. "Buy it. Buy more. Buy the whole damn company, because I will require them to dress you at all times," he mutters as he moves forward.

He has to be joking. "Alexei, I…" I gasp, cut off as he deftly plucks one of the cups of the bra down and his lips latch onto my nipple.

My eyes roll back into my head. I never really saw myself as someone who liked this, but I think maybe I was wrong. *This is incredible,* I think as I arch into his mouth. His other hand is on my thigh, moving up toward where I'm drenched for him as he uses his tongue and teeth to pull on my nipples. I'm writhing against him at this point, desperate for pressure on my clit.

Desperate for something that feels like it's just around the corner.

"Alexei," I whimper.

"I know, milaya. I know," he whispers.

Then his finger is tracing the edge of my panties.

I shiver with anticipation.

Slowly, so slowly it almost hurts, he pushes inside the lace thong that I'm wearing.

I want to scream as his thick finger presses inside me.

This is so much better than before. I bite my tongue, trying my hardest to keep myself from shouting his name as loud as I can.

"Yes," I whisper instead.

"That's so good, Maggie," he sounds reverent as he continues to move. The way he grunts, I can tell that he's having a hard time restraining himself as well. "Are you this wet for me already?"

"Yes," I repeat. I moan as he slides out, the noise obscene in the quiet library.

"You're such a good girl, being ready for me whenever I want you," he whispers into my ear. He licks my neck and I moan.

Alexei groans as well. "Do you like this, milaya? When I tell you how good you are?"

Absolutely, yes, I do. However, I don't trust myself to respond. Alexei is going to know everything about me anyway. He can read me like a book. I just moan and press against him, hoping he will bring me closer to the orgasm that has been haunting me since he first showed me what I'm missing the other day.

I want this.

I know that if we do this, I won't be able to go back. We'll be husband and wife for real, in a way that we haven't been before.

But I'm ready for it.

Suddenly he pulls back, and I cry out. "What are you doing?"

His eyes are dark and hooded with lust. He looks at me, a smirk curling on his lips. "I'm so glad you like your present."

I prop myself up on my elbows, and the movement makes my breasts jiggle. "Of course I do. But I feel like I haven't gotten you anything."

"You are enough," he says softly.

I huff. "But every time I come in here, I'm going to think about you. About this," I gesture to the room. "This is the best gift that anyone has ever given me. How can I repay you?"

"You never have to," he growls.

I shake my head. "But what can I do that would be the same? How will I make sure that I'm always on your mind, too?"

"Because, Maggie," he says softly. "All I think about is you."

For a moment I pause, taken aback by his words.

Then, I smile.

"I want you, Alexei. I want all of you."

He freezes. "Maggie. Are you sure?"

"Yes," I say. I'll beg if I have to. "I need you."

He pauses. If I've learned anything about Alexei in our time together, it's that he doesn't make decisions without thinking about them first.

So I know that right now, all I have to do is wait.

I don't have to wait long, however, because he moves forward.

His hands are everywhere, and I totally forget that I'm just in expensive underwear and a bra. Alexei makes me feel... powerful. Worshiped. Normally, I'd be pretty self-conscious to be spread out on a desk like this.

However, Alexei's eyes immediately bolster my confidence. "Look at you, Maggie," his voice is so low I have to lean forward to make out his words. "You're so fucking beautiful."

I smile and the doubt disappears. In its place, I'm feeling bold and sexy, and I channel that for a moment. Alexei growls when I lay back on his desk and spread my legs open for him. "Please," I whisper to him.

I want him. I want everything. I want this, and I can't wait to possibly have it forever.

Alexei's there in a heartbeat. He still has his pants and shirt on, and he pulls them off slowly. He's standing naked before me, one hand on each of my knees, spreading me wider.

"These are pretty," he says as he traces the center of my soaking panties upwards.

I shiver. "I like that they match."

"I see that. Do you always match?"

"Only when I dress with an audience in mind," I breathe. *Only for you*.

His eyes glimmer with satisfaction, and I think that he understands what I haven't said. He presses my legs closed and hooks a finger in each side of the lacy underwear. I lift my hips up and he slides them down my hips, then drops them on the floor.

"Show me where you want me, Maggie," he whispers.

Slowly, I part my legs again.

Alexei's eyes focus sharply on my center. I know I'm wet. I also know that he likes what he sees, because his eyes go unfocused and slack.

And his already impressive cock jerks, like it's excited to get inside me.

Alexei steps forward, and he pauses.

"Maggie, I don't…"

"It's okay," I pant. "I want… you. Even if there's… well. I mean. We're married and all, right?"

"What does that mean?"

I huff. He's literally pressed right at the edge of where I want him, and I'm getting impatient.

"I don't care if I get pregnant, Alexei. I'd be happy to have a baby with you," I snap.

The words feel loud. But I don't have time to consider his reaction.

Because in the next moment, he pushes inside me, and I'm lost.

We both pant as he fully seats himself. He's big. Not outrageously so, but big enough that I squirm a little at the intrusion. I'm certainly not expecting it to feel quite like…. This.

"Shit. Maggie. I forgot you…"

"I'm fine," I whisper. "I'm actually really good."

"Good?"

I nod.

He makes a movement and I hiss, the full impact of his thick cock a little clearer now than it was before.

He freezes. "Are you okay," I hear him whisper in my ear.

I nod. "Give me a second."

I can count each heartbeat as Alexei waits.

Finally, I'm ready. "Move, please," I say.

His tongue licks the spot behind my ear again, and I tremble. "Anything you want, it's yours," he rumbles.

Then he moves.

Alexei pushes into me and slides out like it's his only purpose in life. It's focused and intense. I'm the center of Alexei's world, and he's the center of mine. I moan as I press upwards, searching for pressure on my clit that will bring the orgasm I'm sitting right against.

"Turn around," he whispers. He pulls out and I obey. I fold over his desk, my hands stretched out in front of me. He steps behind me and kicks my legs apart, his hands gripping my hips in an iron grasp that makes me think I'll probably have bruises in the shape of his fingers tomorrow.

Strangely, the idea doesn't repulse me.

I don't have too much time to think about it though, because once Alexei slides back into me, he steals my breath as he pounds against me. The sound of skin slapping against skin dominates the room, and I renew my grip on the desk, hoping like hell that I can just hold on while Alexei drives us both toward the climax on the horizon.

I'm almost there.

I'm so close. His dick is rubbing against something inside me that feels so incredibly amazing, I close my eyes and wait for bliss.

Alexei roughly grabs my hair and tugs. I get the hint and pull myself up. His arm goes around my torso right under my breasts, and his hand roughly palms one of them as he slams into me. We're close; I can feel him against my back, the relentless pressure of him as he thrusts us both into a climax.

His hand disappears from my hair, and I feel it at my clit. "Come with me, Maggie," he whispers in my ear.

Then he bites my neck. His fingers press on my clit, rubbing in a circle.

And I do as he says.

A wave of orgasm crashes over me. Every nerve in my body lights up, an electric network of nerves and neurons and who knows what else, that ripple through every one of my muscles. I can't help myself; I scream his name.

"Maggie," he snarls against my neck. He repeats my name like a prayer as he shakes behind me.

I smile.

We both pant, the moment changing as we come down.

"Alexei?"

He murmurs. "Hmm?"

"I think this is already the best Christmas I've ever had."

ALEXEI

❄

The storm has long since gone.

The weeks have wound toward the holiday.

And I have not gone back to Novgorod.

How could I?

Everything that I have ever wanted, everything that I ever could want...

It is here.

I can't believe that there was a time where I thought a wife would not add something to my life.

Clearly, I was a fool.

Because the days I have spent with Maggie, the nights we have cherished each other?

I have not felt such joy since...

Well.

Since I last spent a Christmas in Orlov House.

However, it is not just the fact that I am here for the holiday that makes it feel so.

It is the fact that I am here with her.

Everything Maggie touches turns into sunshine. Her laughter elevates the rooms, changing their fading paints and the dour faces of my ancestors into a tapestry of joy. The way she thinks of the world, the endless information she has to give me, it provides a wonderful background to whatever I do as we move around the house.

I have not taken a business meeting since I came to Orlov House. I may never take one again.

Truly, that is how marvelous my time with Maggie is.

We wake up and discover things in the home. We look behind curtains. We dig out boxes that Elena scolds us for getting into, then rolls her eyes as we look at them anyway.

I have never known more about my own home than I do right now, and I do not think that in my life, I would have ever wanted to know as much about this house as I do now.

But now, it does not just feel like my house.

It feels like *our* home.

And that makcs all the difference.

Maggie has put my finances to good use. Every day, new packages and parcels appear at the front door. Some contain clothes, which I am happy to provide for her. Maggie has excellent taste, and I can already tell that she will start trends wherever she goes.

Some contain more delicate items. That I am more than happy to reveal.

Today, on the day before the holiday, I finally have a box that I am going to surprise her with.

I can't wait to show it to her.

It does not slip my mind that I have not yet actually *asked* her to marry me. In all of this, Maggie has had no choice but to choose me.

I think that over the past few weeks, I have done a reasonably good job of helping her to choose me.

My vision now is to ensure that she does.

And, that she feels wonderous in doing so.

I have one last surprise up my sleeve before I give her the final present. I have contacted Koslov, her father, and have arranged for him and her mother to come and spend the actual day of Christmas with us. They will remain at Orlov House through the New Year, so that we Russians can fully celebrate our favorite holiday, and then they will return to the United States.

In an effort to make her happy, I wish to do this.

Her mother is ecstatic. It is also clear to me that her father has rediscovered some kind of connection with her, as I had them on the video call and I could see the glances he sent her way.

I'm not sure how to handle that, but I'm sure that Maggie and I will work it out upon their arrival.

I do not need her father's permission to give Maggie the gift I wish to give her. I technically already have it, as we have been married for weeks now.

However, I know that it would matter to Maggie to have her mother here for the holiday.

And thus.

They will arrive.

The weather, for once, is cooperating. There will not even be a chance of snow to ruin the surprise that I have planned.

Everything, finally, is perfect.

Maggie follows me down the hallway to my mother's room. This, too, is part of the plan.

But it is the part that I am most nervous about.

She lingers outside of the door.

I turn.

"Alexei," she whispers, her eyes wide as she takes in the room. "Look, we don't have to..."

"Please," I murmur. "Come in."

Meekly, she follows.

Inside, I gesture to the furniture, asking her to pull one side of the sheet on the covered item nearest to us. Slowly, we pull each one off, coughing as dust swirls through the air.

I pile the large canvas sheets in a corner, then look around the room.

My heart catches in my throat. It's exactly as I left it.

Even her vanity still has her jewelry box out on it.

I walk nearer, my fingers itching to touch the necklaces in there. To smell the perfume bottle that still holds something of her scent.

I turn.

Maggie is looking at me. I can tell she wants to ask me questions, but I shake my head.

This, too, is something that I want to give her.

"My mother died when I was a teenager," I declare. It's the easiest way to say it, and while I know she is already aware, it's still the easiest place to begin.

"I lived with her, here, in Orlov House. My father lived here too, but he was often away on business. Our time at Orlov House was... fun. Elena was here, as was much of the rest of the staff. The village, the house, the grounds... they were my playground," I murmur.

Maggie nods, her lips tilting into a smile. "You really were a little prince."

I snort. "In the sense that I was spoiled, yes. My mother was a good mother, she ensured that I had a bit of humility. However, it was awfully hard for the staff to not treat me like I was a prince. Which made me into somewhat of a tyrant, I warrant," I laugh.

She shakes her head. "I'm certain you were just an average kid, Alexei."

"You'll have to ask Elena, but I highly doubt it," I mutter.

Maggie rolls her eyes, but I pull her close, tugging her down onto one of the comfortable couches. I swear, I can still smell my mother on the fabric, and it makes my chest ache.

This next part of the story is far less pleasant.

"I didn't know she was sick until the doctors came and told

me that there wouldn't be another Christmas for her," I whisper.

Maggie goes very, very still.

"My father wasn't here. It was just me and her. I don't know if the doctor thought through his proclamation, but as soon as he walked away, he told me that my mother's illness would be fatal. He told me to send for my father."

"Alexei…"

"I did," I grit. "I asked for him immediately."

"What happened then?"

"He came. We sat with her until she passed. It was a terrible time, because I had relatives come to pay their respects and they treated it like it was almost… a reunion. Orlov House was full, and the sounds of chatter and laughter were the background to my mother's death," I whisper.

"Oh, Alexei," Maggie says.

I shake my head. "When she died, my father asked me what I wanted to do with Orlov House. I told him nothing. At the time, I wanted to see the whole thing off. I wanted it all to disappear."

"But you didn't let it."

I shake my head. "No. I went to live with my father in Moscow. He passed recently as well, but it was not the same as when mother died. We, he and I both, were not the same after she died."

Maggie takes my hand.

I marvel at her fingers, the fine bones of her wrist and the flow of them into her small arm. I tug her close, tucking her head against my shoulder.

"Orlov House has always been the last place that I saw my mother. Until now, I had only remembered the pain. The loss, the way that I lost not just her, but my entire childhood as well," I whisper.

Maggie doesn't say anything. She listens, patiently, and I take a deep breath.

"I have never wanted to lose Orlov House. But I have also avoided it. I don't come home for holidays. I don't spend New Year here. I try to talk to Elena, but I don't see her, because I don't come back here," I whisper. "I knew I needed a wife to maintain the house, but I refused to actually find a wife. Because if I found a wife, then I would need to face the house as well."

"I kind of figured that's why you wanted to leave," Maggie smiles.

I pull her close. "You are too smart, my Maggie."

"I'm just smart enough, and I also know a lot about how people avoid their problems."

I laugh.

"Maggie. Magdalena. You have shown me that I cut myself off from the memories of Orlov House, but in the process, I did too much. I cut off the memories of my happiness with my mother as well. Being here with you has reminded me that I am more than just the man my father made me. I am also the man my mother made me. You reminded me of this, and that is the greatest gift anyone could have ever given."

She pulls back, a smile curling across her lips. "I love that, Alexei."

"And I l—"

I'm not able to finish the sentence.

Maggie's eyes flash with a panic and she quickly moves in, her lips bruising mine. For a second, I'm startled. I wanted to confess how I feel, and it seems almost like she guessed that.

It seems like she suspected what I was about to say, and then decided that she didn't want to hear it.

But that can't be the case.

I return Maggie's kiss. It grows heated, and my mind blanks. I pull her on top of me, letting her sweet, tight body straddle mine as our kisses grow fervent. My hands race over her skin, and her lips caress mine. Soon, I don't remember what I was going to say.

All I want to do is show her how I feel. Show her the depths of my heart.

There will be time enough for us to talk. I have a lifetime, after all, to show Maggie how much she means to me.

As we sink into each other, my doubts are soothed.

Maggie is mine.

And she will be ready to hear that.

Eventually.

❄

Later, when we are tucked into the luxurious bed in my room, a fire crackling at our feet, my doubt returns.

Why did Maggie cut me off?

I am easily distracted, it would seem, but Maggie is not… duplicitous. We have always promised to be honest with each other. It's one of the foundations of our tentative, if happy, relationship.

So why did she keep my truth from coming out?

I want to wake her, but I know that would not be the best solution. She's sleeping peacefully at that, and I cannot worry about such matters.

Maggie feels for me as much as I feel for her. I know it.

There's no other reason why she would treat me so well. We've spent the past few weeks wrapped in each other's arms, a haze of cookies and treats and holiday cheer that's so thick, now I'm wondering if it was just a fog.

Just something that made me miss the signs of what was really going on with her.

The urge to look at her phone, to see what she's telling her mother, flashes over me. That would be a violation of her privacy, and I clench my fists instead.

Besides, her mother would not have agreed to come and visit if she was concerned for her daughter's feelings or safety.

At least, I don't think she would have.

The doubts compel me to stand. I walk to the window, looking out. The darkness around Orlov House is intense. Aside from the decorative lighting on the walls of the ancient manor house, there is no additional light until you reach the village, and then barely anything until Novgorod, which is a long enough drive that you really can't see the lights leading that direction.

Most of the time, I find the solitude completely unremarkable.

Today, however, it makes me itch.

Will Maggie be willing to accept this? Will she be able to accept the life that I have to offer her? I am rich. I am powerful.

But she has no need for wealth or power. Maggie has something that many of us spend our whole life trying to find money and power to fill.

She has happiness.

Joy.

She has the ability to make both of those things wherever she goes, because she is not desperately scraping at the wounds of her childhood, trying to glue them together as an adult.

Does she really feel for me as I do for her?

I'm deeply enmeshed in musing when my phone lights up. I tiptoe over to it, grabbing it, and I raise it to my face.

Anatoly: Boss. It's been about an hour, and there's no sign of your in-laws.

A chill skates down my spine.

Me: What do the officers say?

Anatoly: They won't tell me.

Fuck.

A dozen scenarios, each one of them worse than the next, crash over me. It's highly possible that Kozlov's enemies have finally found him.

Which would mean that our perfect Christmas would not be so perfect after all.

In fact.

It would be ruined.

And since I want it to be perfect, that will not do.

With one last look at a sleeping Maggie, I turn to dress.

She needs me to protect her. To protect her family.

It's time to be the bigger monster.

MAGGIE

Alexei isn't there when I wake up.

I know it shouldn't bother me. There's nothing to worry about. Not really.

But after last night, his absence makes me feel just a little confused, and really, really nervous.

I roll over in bed. My first instinct is to text him and ask him where he is, but I pause on that.

I don't want to be a clingy, needy wife.

We haven't established communication for things like absences yet. I know that he said at some point in the last few weeks that he did most of his work in Novgorod, but surely he would have told me that he was going back there before he left.

And, it's Christmas morning.

He wouldn't leave on Christmas morning.

Right?

Unless he's pissed at you for last night.

I huff out a long breath.

Okay. I did cut him off on purpose last night. He was so sweet, and I know that he wanted to tell me that he loved me.

But the same reservation that I had about it popped into my mind.

It's too soon to love him.

I didn't want him to tell me that he loved me. Not yet.

Because if he tells me too soon, it might not be real.

However, it did kind of ruin the moment. Even after we had sex, which was great like it always is, he still seemed... distant.

Did he though?

I flop my arms in frustration. Alexei is a really sweet man. I honestly can't really decide if he was actually distant, or if I just made it up because I was nervous about him seeming distant.

This is why you're never supposed to therapize yourself, Mags.

Bleh.

I lean up. I should go look for him, but I am kind of hurt.

Alexei knows how important Christmas is to me. The fact that he's not here right now, and he didn't leave a note?

It kind of sucks.

This is why it's too soon to say you love each other, dummy. You don't even really know him.

That thought settles like lead in my chest.

It's true, though. The past couple of weeks have been great, but they don't really mean anything. You don't know someone until you see them live their life, after all. And, even then, sometimes you can never really know someone.

And that makes me feel suddenly, and intensely, lonely.

I resolve to make the best of this situation. It's Christmas, and no matter what Alexei is doing, I'm going to have a good day.

Elena is off today. She told me that she's spending the day with a niece in Moscow. The other staff are not necessarily required to attend.

So it's just me.

Alone.

In Orlov House.

The loneliness is back, punching me down like bread dough.

I swallow back my disappointment, and instead decide to take a shower.

I do my best to keep my mind in the present and try to enjoy the hot shower spray against my skin, but I can't help it. My mind wanders a little, because every shower I've had for the past few weeks has either been with Alexei, or in view of him.

Or because of him, in a couple of remarkably sticky situations.

He's coming back. It's okay, you just don't know him very well. He's probably been called away to work or something.

It doesn't matter how often I tell myself the words, I'm still trying to say them to cover up the anxiety that's coursing through me.

Breakfast is lonely. The house creaks and groans, but other than that, the silence feels deafening.

I kind of feel like I'm hearing things. Voices. Sounds.

So when the front door opens— a creaking, shattering sound — for a minute I'm not certain that it's real.

Until I hear voices, actual human voices, as well.

I nearly stumble over my feet as I run down to the main entryway.

Breathless, I slide around the corner. "Alexei?" I pant.

There are three people in the doorway.

Alexei.

A shape that it takes a second for me to register as my father.

And...

My mother.

I'm not sure why, but the second I see her, I burst into tears.

The propensity is clearly genetic, because she does the same. We collide, crashing into each other, and we slide to the floor, sobbing.

Behind her, I hear Alexei mutter something to my father in Russian. I really should learn the language, but I wouldn't be able to figure it out now even if I tried.

My mother is here.

In my arms. In the foyer of Orlov House.

And I've never been happier.

Eventually, we manage to pull ourselves together. I wipe my eyes and look at them. "What the heck? How are you here?"

My mother and... father (again, it's kind of weird to describe him as that, but he technically did contribute the genetic material that makes him my biological father) exchange a look.

A very intimate, somewhat telling look.

"How about you and I go talk for a second, baby?" my mom says with a smile.

I glance at Alexei, but he's looking away from me.

My heart sinks.

"Okay, um. Thanks, mom. And uh...dad," I say.

I can't believe that I said it.

I don't think he can either. His eyes go wide, and he looks at my mom like he's asking for permission.

Her little nod gives me a lot of questions.

"Come on, mom. Let me show you around," I whisper.

I grab my mom's hand. We walk down the hall.

It's time to figure out what's going on.

❇

"Okay so. Spill."

We manage to make it to the kitchen, but beyond that, nothing yet. I hand my mom a cookie, and she bites into it.

"Oh honey. These are way better than mine!"

"So not the point, mom."

My mom sighs. "Okay. Well. Where do you want to start?"

"What are you doing here?"

She waves a hand. "Oh, that's easy. Your husband contacted your father and asked for us to come for Christmas."

"And you... just... you said yes?"

"Well of course. Why wouldn't we?"

I pause.

My mom stares at me for a minute longer, then understanding dawns. "Oh. That's what you're worried about."

"What?"

"You like him. A lot."

"I..."

She waves a hand. "I gave birth to you, Magdalena. I know that face. You really like him. I think you probably love him. But you, for some reason, are keeping yourself from admitting it."

"I am not."

Laughing, she walks around the island and pulls me into a hug. "You, my love, have the same look on your face as you did whenever you picked me up a cake from the bakery. You absolutely want to eat all of it, but you know that you shouldn't."

I sigh. "Mom. It's just not logical. I mean, do I feel a lot for him right now? Yes, but it can't be what I think it is because—"

"You love him, sweetheart. You don't have to hide it from me."

I think I know what I'm going to do for my master's thesis. Because someone needs to study the phenomenon of what happens to a person when their mom says, out loud, the thing that they've been trying to hide from themselves.

Bursting into tears, I bury my head in her shoulder. "I can't love him," I say, gasping around the tears that are pouring out of me. "I haven't been around him enough to love him."

"Sweetheart. Love isn't logical. It doesn't always mean you've been with someone for their whole life," my mom gently pats my back. "I mean, I fell in love with your dad that night."

"And he left you!"

Wow.

That brings on a whole new wave of tears.

Eventually, I calm down a little. I wipe my eyes and pull back, bringing in deep, shuddering breaths.

My mom's eyes are wet too.

"He did leave us, baby. But he also didn't. He tried to stay, but he couldn't. They would have found us a lot earlier and tried to kill us, and I didn't have a snowball's chance in hell of surviving them with a baby on my hip. He did what he did to keep us alive, and now…"

"You forgive him?" I ask.

It comes out as more of an accusation than I meant, and my mom's face pales.

I sigh. "Mom…"

"I don't know if I fully forgive him. I think that there's been a lot of time, and a lot of space, that he could have probably figured out a better solution. Twenty-three years is a long time, and I wish he had stepped in sooner," she whispers.

"Amen," I snort.

My mom's lips curl up. "But, the past few weeks, I've remembered a lot about your dad. Including the fact that I like him. A lot. And I loved him the second I laid eyes on him a little over twenty-three years ago."

"How?" I whisper.

She shrugs. "I'm not sure, baby. But all of that came roaring back as soon as we started talking again, and I'm not going to deny those feelings."

I look to the side, refusing to acknowledge her slight jab.

"Alexei is a good man. He asked me to come here for you. He wants you to be happy, baby. His reputation is practically made of platinum. I get feelings about people, you know this, and I have a good feeling about this one."

I nibble my lip. "But what if he has to… leave. Like dad?"

She shrugs. "Then you'll come live with me. But I have a feeling that your life with Alexei Orlov is going to be just a little different than your dad's life, my love."

"Why?"

My mom sighs, then gestures wildly to the house. "This is not the type of house that a man has when he's under any kind of threat."

"It's been in his family for like… hundreds of years."

She makes an exaggerated face. "No. You don't say."

I shove her lightly on the shoulder. "Also, he's kind of a prince."

"Your dad told me that. I also mentioned that you've been a princess for as long as I've known you, so it's kind of fitting."

I laugh, glad that the tears feel like they're behind me.

"Maggie?"

I look up, smiling at my mom.

She takes my face in her hands. I lean in, relishing the feeling of her soft palms on my cheeks. I close my eyes, just sitting and enjoying the fact that she's here. She's safe.

And she's with me.

"I think it's time that you ditch the whole princess thing."

My eyes pop open. "What? Why?"

My mom's mouth curls into a smile.

"Because I think Alexei is ready to treat you like a queen."

❄

Mom and I wander back to the main living room, where Alexei and my dad are softly conversing in Russian. When we walk into the room, my dad's whole body changes. His eyes light up when he looks at my mom, and when he looks at me?

There's something like hope there.

"This house is freaking incredible," my mom says. "Don't you want a tour, love?"

My dad looks somewhat stern, his eyes bouncing between Alexei and me. "I..."

"Come with me. Now. I think I can even find our room," my mom mutters.

Finally taking the hint, my dad allows himself to be dragged from the room.

Leaving Alexei and I, standing in front of the Christmas tree.

For some reason, this feels...

Awkward.

I glance up at Alexei, who is studying me.

Where do I start? Do I say that I'm sorry for doubting him? Sorry for cutting him off? Do I thank him for getting my parents? Do I...

"I'm sorry I left without telling you," he says.

I tilt my head.

"There was some issue with customs. Anatoly texted me, and I needed to leave to solve the problem."

"Is everything okay?" I whisper.

He nods. "Your father's visa was old. However, it was nothing that I couldn't fix."

My lips curl. "The bigger monster."

"In this case, just the richer one."

I notice that he still seems...

Distant.

Well.

Here goes.

I take a deep breath. "Look, about last night. I wanted to tell you that I'm—"

Alexei puts his finger over my lips, and I pause.

"Wait. Just... Wait..." he whispers.

Uh.

Okay?

I freeze.

Alexei runs around the Christmas tree. He pulls one of the lower branches aside and grabs a little wrapped package.

My heart starts to beat faster, and he brings me the box.

"Here," he says.

"Alexei. I didn't get you anything—"

"Please, milaya," he whispers. "Open it."

Silently, I grab the box. My hands shake as I tug at the wrapping. He used a really beautiful red paper that's shot through with strands of curling silver.

"Did you wrap this yourself?"

Alexei's mouth tilts into a grin, and some of the playful man that I've come to love over the last few weeks is there again.

The sight gives me hope.

"You definitely did a pretty good job with it," I murmur as I continue to struggle with the wrapping. Eventually, though, I manage to get it off, and it falls onto the floor.

The box is small.

But I kind of recognize it.

I mean. Not this specific box.

But I know what boxes that look like this mean.

Hands shaking, I pull the box open.

I can't help the gasp that emerges when I finally see the contents.

My eyes snap up to Alexei's. "Alexei.... I...I don't..."

"Do you like them?"

That makes me squeeze out a small, nervous giggle.

Like them?

Sitting in the box are two of the most beautiful rings that I've ever seen in my life. One is an engagement ring that's literally the size of a chunk of ice. The diamond in the middle is a pale, ice-blue, and it's surrounded by so many smaller diamonds that my eyes kind of hurt as they catch the sparkle from the Christmas tree.

The other ring is a wedding band. It's gorgeous. It clearly matches the ring, and it's crusted with small diamonds, each one cut into a slightly different shape. It should look chaotic, but the overall effect as they balance against each other is one of harmony and cohesion.

Together, they're absolutely stunning.

"Milaya?"

I shake my head. "Alexei. These are the most beautiful rings that I've ever seen in my whole life. But how..."

He gets down on one knee, and my heart stops.

Gently, Alexei takes the rings from the box. He takes my trembling hand and slips one, then the other, onto my finger.

"Maggie. Magdalena. My love. My heart. You did not choose me as your husband. If you could have, I have no doubt you wouldn't have chosen me. Before I met you, I was... a beast," he mutters.

I give him a smile. "Hardly. A monster, maybe, but you've never been a beast."

He chuckles, pressing a kiss on my knuckles. "I was someone, certainly. I was someone who didn't believe that he needed a wife, or love, or any of that. I required a wife in order to maintain my dominance over my family legacy, but I didn't think that I needed one. I was content to pass every day in my business. To remain in Novgorod forever, to let Orlov House remain empty."

I feel like crying. But I refuse to.

Alexei stands, tugging me close. "You, Maggie, reminded me that Orlov House is never meant to be empty. It is a house for a family. A house for love. A house for people to live their lives within. It isn't a mausoleum, and I cannot honor my mother without making it live again. You taught me that life is meant to be lived, not endured. I love you," he whispers.

My breath catches in my throat.

"I love you. And I think you stopped me from saying it last night, and while I don't understand why..."

"I love you too," I gush.

Alexei blinks like I said something much worse.

"I love you. I'm sorry about last night. I told myself that it couldn't be real, that I couldn't love you so quickly, but screw it. I love you, Alexei Orlov," I say through the tears that I definitely have no control over anymore.

"You love me?"

"Yes," I breathe.

Alexei sweeps in, sealing his mouth over mine in a kiss.

Everything is in that kiss. Every moment of joy we've experienced. Every thing we've said.

Every truth we've exchanged.

When he pulls back, he smiles. "Your parents are still indisposed, I assume."

I wrinkle my nose. "I am absolutely not going to find out."

Alexei nods. "I meant to ask you this in front of your parents, but the time seems better now. Maggie, will you choose me? Will you be my wife, for now, and for all the Christmas holidays to come?"

The smile that splits my face feels as bright as the star on the top of the tree.

"I love you, Alexei Orlov. I love you, and I'll choose you this Christmas, and every Christmas after."

When he pulls me into a kiss this time, we're both crying happy tears. He sweeps me into a hug, and I laugh, shouting my joy into the walls of the house that surround us like a warm hug.

Alexei Orlov isn't a monster. He's a miracle.

And he's all mine.

EPILOGUE: ONE YEAR LATER

Maggie

"Alexei. If you put any more tinsel on that tree, it's going to fall over."

I laugh as Alexei turns. It's night, and the house is finally asleep. We're hosting a lot more people this year. My mom and dad, of course, because they live with us full time now. Not in Orlov House, but in one of the minor houses down in the village. Alexei has relatives coming in this year too, because we decided that this year, we're going to bring back one of the traditions from his mom's time.

We're having a huge Christmas party.

"Well. I suppose I am a little… enthusiastic," he mutters.

Alexei steps back, dusting his hands off on his soft pants. "Come, Milaya," he murmurs.

I step into his arms, sighing as he tucks me under his arm.

We survey the tree…

EPILOGUE: ONE YEAR LATER

Together.

It's beautiful. We've made some changes from last year, including putting his mother's portrait over the fire, so she can join the party.

I swear she smiles in the sparkling light.

"Milaya, are you ready for this?" Alexei murmurs.

Most of the guests will finish arriving tomorrow, which is going to be amazing.

"I'm ready," I say.

I turn to look at Alexei. "Are you?"

He wrinkles his nose. "And share you with so many people? No."

I laugh. "You don't have to share me. I'm all yours, my love," I murmur.

He pulls my hand to his lips and kisses it.

I love this. I love him.

Alexei is perfect for me.

His blue eyes flash a little. "I have something for you."

"You do?"

"Come with me," he murmurs.

I laugh. Alexei really does love to give gifts. I'm definitely not going to complain, so I follow him down the many hallways of Orlov House to our room.

Inside, the bed is neatly made...

But there's a black box on it.

I look at him, curiosity in my eyes. "We said we weren't going to do gifts this year!"

Alexei always says no gifts. Then he always gets them.

But this time, I'm prepared.

I'm going to be the one surprising him with a gift this year.

"See what's inside, milaya."

Curious, I step forward. I put my hands on the box, and slide it closer.

Alexei moves behind me, kissing the side of my neck. I smile and shut my eyes, leaning into his kiss.

"This is not a gift we will share. This is for us. Just for you... and just for me," he whispers.

I open my eyes and gasp, his kiss hitting me like a shot of straight adrenaline. My hands shake slightly as I pull the black cardboard closer to take a look inside.

Alexei always has this effect on me. I take a minute to compose myself before I pull the lid off of the box.

"No wrapping this year?" I tease.

He shakes his head, and I look down.

My jaw drops.

It's a box of sex toys.

My heart pounds as I look them over. "Alexei," I murmur as I pick up a glass dildo. "This... how.... Did you remember that I said I wanted to try these?"

I liked my vibrator, and a few months ago, I had mentioned to Alexei that I might be interested in more toys.

EPILOGUE: ONE YEAR LATER

"Of course I did. Merry Christmas Alexei," he says with a laugh. He slides to the bed in front of me, and tugs at my flowy cotton pants.

I sit on the bed and let him pull them off as I examine the other items in the box. "I.. I don't really know where to start." I look away, hiding my blush.

"Well. That makes sense, milaya. I thought we could decide together," Alexei rasps. He moves to stand between my legs, and moves the box next to me on the bed, where he can access them. He cups my chin and brings my face to his. The redness across my chest creeps up in my cheeks, and I gaze adoringly into his eyes.

It's strange, to feel like I'm caught right now. I'm definitely curious about the box...

But I also feel a little vulnerable right now.

However, there's no one I would rather feel more vulnerable with than Alexei.

He tugs at my face until I meet his gaze. His eyes are warm and soft, and he rubs his thumb along my jaw in a familiar soothing gesture. "We don't have to do anything you don't want to," he reassures me.

"It's not that," I say with a sigh. My throat works, but I don't want to say that I am embarrassed about not knowing what to start with, or how to use them. He waits patiently for me to continue. God, he's always so patient with me.

Alexei is the best man on the face of the planet. I'll never think otherwise.

And, I owe him an answer.

"I don't know what to do," I whisper.

EPILOGUE: ONE YEAR LATER

I really do want to use more toys, but I don't know where to start, and the box is…

Well. It's kind of intimidating.

Alexei folds me into his arms and hugs me close. As I have for the last year, I sag into his warm chest.

"Maggie?"

"Yeah?"

"We will go as slow as you need. I want to show you how very, very good this can feel. Would you like me to show you?"

I pull back and the tension inside me unfurls a little.

Alexei is undoubtedly the love of my life. He always makes me feel better. Through the past year, we've come across many challenges. Neither of us knows the answers to everything, but Alexei is so good at keeping calm and making me feel like I can do anything, it doesn't really matter.

It's been a heck of a year.

But with Alexei, I can take on anything.

And I am really freaking excited to try this.

Especially with him.

"How did you pick which ones to order?" I ask as I study the box again.

He shrugs. "I just went with one of each category."

My lips curl into a smile. "You just randomly clicked on one?"

Alexei's cheeks get a little red. Well. It looks like I've done the impossible, and gotten under the skin of my cool-as-a-cucumber husband. "Milaya, I picked the highest rated one in

EPILOGUE: ONE YEAR LATER

each category," he says a little defensively. "I got so distracted thinking about you using them that I could not possibly choose just one."

I laugh and put a quick peck on his cheek. "Thank you, Alexei."

"No, milaya. The thanks are all mine. Now. Are you ready?"

I wink at him. "Let's see what toys you put in my stocking, love."

I lay back down on our bed, and pull my soft cotton pants off all the way. His attention focuses in on me with laser-like intensity and goosebumps break out over my skin. I hook a finger in my panties and slowly pull them down my legs.

I can feel his eyes track the whole way.

Over the last year, I've gotten a lot bolder. I like it.

Alexei *loves* it.

His stare is something I've gotten used to, and I have to say, it's part of the game now.

I sigh, pretending to be unaffected by the weight of his focus, and shrug. "I guess we should just pick one and see how it goes."

Alexi's eyes go molten. They take on that hungry look that I love so much to see as he scours my naked body. I let my legs fall open, showing him my center and where I am so incredibly wet for him.

He scrubs a hand over his mouth as he looks. "God, milaya. You're so fucking pretty."

I move a hand down toward my core, loving how he watches

EPILOGUE: ONE YEAR LATER

every second of the journey. "Pick one, Alexei," I repeat huskily.

He blinks like he's trying to gather his thoughts. With wide pupils that never leave mine, his hand gropes in the box and pulls out the glass dildo that I was a little intimidated by earlier. Dimly, I notice it has a unique shape and color.

I laugh. "Alexei, is that shaped like a candy cane?"

"It's festive," he says hoarsely, and I laugh even as I swirl my fingers around my clit. Alexei, still fully clothed, tucks the glass into his waistband. He puts his shirt over it. I tilt my head at him in curiosity.

"To warm it up," he explains. "It's too cold right now. I don't want you to feel uncomfortable."

I shiver, because part of me wonders what it would feel like cold. However, given how truly dismal the Russian winter can be, I realize that he probably is right. I nod and arch for him, showing my body's features.

It's a good thing he hasn't noticed how they're changing...

Yet.

"Touch me, Alexei," I whisper.

He obeys.

Alexei falls on my breasts like he's starving. He pulls the delicate cups of my lingerie down and licks my nipples into stiff peaks. Gently, he bites the underside of my breasts. I moan as his hand covers mine, playing with my clit as he teases my nipples into tender points. "You're so wet for me, Maggie. So wet, and it's all mine," he growls.

I shiver.

EPILOGUE: ONE YEAR LATER

His words always take my arousal from simmering to nuclear within seconds. That's the other thing. Alexei is always restrained. Even when he's angry, I've never seen him really lose his cool.

But in bed, I can make him lose his cool. I make him turn into a possessive nightmare.

A possessive nightmare that I absolutely freaking love.

"You're such a good girl, Maggie. You'll do anything for me, won't you?"

"Yes," I purr as his tongue lashes over my neck.

"You want to see what this box can do for you, pretty Maggie?"

I shudder. His dirty talk always gets me. "*Yes,*" I moan.

He leans back and grabs the glass candy cane dildo from his waistband. Slowly, he presses it to my entrance. "Do you want any lube, baby?"

"No," I whisper. The glass is still slightly chilly, and I can feel it stretching my entrance. I know it will slide in without a problem, because my arousal is always off the charts when Alexei and I go for it like this.

I thought it would get old.

And it never has.

"Okay," Alexei says. He presses it inside me. My eyes watch the red and white glass disappear into my body, and Alexei's face takes on a pained look. "Fuck, Maggie. That's so incredible."

He pulls it back out and my eyes nearly roll back in my head at how freaking good it felt.

"Alexei, that feels amazing," I moan. I don't feel him moving, so I open my eyes.

He's staring at me. His face looks almost gaunt with hunger, and he stares at where the toy is embedded in my core.

"Fuck yourself with it," he commands in a low voice that makes me ache for him.

Well.

I did say that I've gotten bolder over the past year.

I reach down and grab the curve of the dildo. Slowly, I push it into me. It makes a wet noise that has both of us moaning, and I draw it out just as slowly.

Alexei curses in Russian, and from what I can gather, he's doing his best to hold on to his control. "Maggie. I can see your wetness all over it."

I don't say anything, but arch my back and repeat the motion. Alexei doesn't move. He watches me as I move the toy in and out of myself, slowly learning the boundaries of where I can press it and where I can't. The curved handle is delightfully easy to just hook a finger in, and with every thrust I grow more and more slick. The noises my body makes as the glass goes in and out of me are bordering on obscene, but it feels so freaking good that I'm not self-conscious at all.

And the whole time, Alexei just watches.

"Do you like it?" I whisper after a while. I'm not self-conscious, but he hasn't moved in minutes. I'm worried, suddenly, that something is off.

"Oh, Maggie," he moans. He stands and I can see his thick cock outlined against his dress pants. "You are doing so fucking well. I have never seen anything sexier than you taking that fucking glass candy cane."

I should laugh. It's an absurd image. But the way Alexei's eyes consume me, I know there is nothing funny about the situation.

I keep going, working myself into a near fever state. "Alexei," I groan. "I want to come, but I... I don't think I can."

The words take a second to sink in, but as soon as they do, Alexei moves like lightning. His hand shoots into the box and pulls out a small vibrator. His hands shake as he finds the power button, and I hear the vibrator buzz. He presses it against my clit and I nearly pass out at the sensation. It's a little too much, and I squirm.

"Is that good, baby?" His voice is so concerned, and love for him washes over me all again.

"No," I whisper. "A little too hard."

He backs off slightly, and starts to move the head of the toy on my clit in a circle. I gasp as electricity shoots up my spine. "There," I grit out.

Alexei listens. The pressure is perfect, and I can feel my orgasm spreading across my low belly. My muscles start to shake, and I close my eyes. I pull the candy cane dildo out of me as my climax builds, and I'm almost there...

Alexei pulls the vibrator off of my clit, and I nearly scream.

"No!" I moan. I prop myself up on my elbows to look at him. "I'm so close!"

"I told you to fuck yourself with it," he says, staring at where the dildo hangs from my fingers. "Not to stop."

EPILOGUE: ONE YEAR LATER

"You..." I sit up on my elbows, but Alexei lightly collars my neck with his hand and pushes me back down.

"You want to come, milaya?" He growls at me.

I nod.

"Then do what I say."

It's a command, plain and simple.

This is new for us. I'm not sure that I like it, but the twinkling of Alexei's warm and happy self sparkles in his eyes as he stares me down.

This isn't just anyone.

This is *Alexei*.

And I want to please him.

I nod, slowly pressing the dildo into my soaking core. Alexei watches. His lips quirk into a smile. "Good girl," he says.

Oh.

Well I do like that.

The buzz of the vibrator fills my ears again, and he presses the vibrator back against me with that same light pressure as before. "Keep going," he grunts.

I do.

It takes about six more pumps of the dildo before I come.

I scream his name when I do.

My limbs are numb after. I lay limp on our bed. I feel Alexei pull the dildo out of me, and shudder as it caresses my tender flesh. I might have drifted off to sleep, because the next thing I know I'm under a blanket and Alexei's arms are around me.

EPILOGUE: ONE YEAR LATER

"Alexei," I mumble as I stretch against him.

"Merry Christmas, Milaya," he murmurs.

That reminds me.

Stirring, I prop myself up on my elbows and squint at him. "Do you need um... anything?"

He shakes his head.

I know that he's probably sporting the erection to end all erections, but Alexei is like that. Sometimes, he just wants to watch me. He wants to make sure that I'm taken care of, first.

It's why I know he's going to be a great dad.

Taking a huge breath, I steel myself for the courage about what's going to come next.

I send a silent prayer up to his mother, who I hope didn't exactly *watch* what we just did, but I hope she's watching over us and giving me the courage I need.

I roll over onto my stomach. "I have something for you."

Alexei's lips tuck into a frown. "Milaya, you are not supposed to get me a gift."

"Okay, that seems like the pot calling the kettle black a little, sir."

"My gift was a gift for the both of us," he says smugly, tucking my face into his shoulder.

I giggle as he kisses the side of my neck. "Alexei. Seriously. This is a present for both of us too. Kind of," I say.

He pulls back. "Well. If it is for the both of us, milaya, then please. Do tell me."

I take a huge breath. I grab one of Alexei's hands, and pull it down, running his warm fingers past my breasts and all the way until I stop it right on top of my belly.

His eyes darken. "Milaya, I told you, I don't need—"

"I'm pregnant," I whisper.

It takes Alexei a second to figure out what I said. I wonder if I should repeat it in Russian, because he seems to be struggling to process.

Then, when he realizes, his eyes go wide. "Maggie," he croaks. "Really?"

"Really," I whisper.

His jaw drops. Then, his eyes widen with fear. "But we just..."

"I'm pretty new," I whisper. "It's not like the baby knows, or anything."

"The baby..." his voice gets thick. His eyes look up to mine. "Our baby."

"Yes, Alexei. Our baby," I whisper.

I squeak when he tugs me close, pressing a huge kiss on my lips. His hand on my belly trembles.

"Milaya?"

"Yes?" I ask.

"You are the best gift. I love you," he whispers.

I smile, pressing my lips to his.

"I love you too."

❄

EPILOGUE: ONE YEAR LATER

Thank you for reading Maggie and Alexei's story, Please leave me a review they help me succeed as an independent author.

If you haven't read A Dark Mafia Christmas: Emmett and Mary's story get it now. If you have, then get ready to lose some sleep on this next spicy drama filled dark and dangerous Bratva King's Secret Twins. Meet Gwen an innocent smart and sassy law student who had to drop out to work and help her family. Nikolai- her dark, and dangerous knight. See who falls first and hard...

Chapter 1

Gwen

"Well goddamn, darlin', you keep spinning like that you might just take my whole paycheck," Jacob, a regular with graying hair and a worn smile, yells to me.

I roll my hips, arching my back while I slide down the pole. My black curls cascade over my shoulder, and a sultry smile spreads across my lips.

"Baby," I purr, swinging my hair over my shoulder. I slide to the floor and crawl closer to the balding man holding a wad of 5's, "it'll be the best check you've ever spent."

He howls like a maniac, and his friends happily shower me with bills. *That's right, keep them coming. Your paycheck will definitely put me ahead of payments for Mason.*

I lean back, letting the pink light from above wash over me. The music fades, and Justin's sorry-ass voice comes over the loudspeaker. "Give it up for the delicious Cinnamon!" I roll back on my heels, licking my lips at the older men. "But hold onto your bulges, boys, because next up is a sweet little slice of heaven. Welcome Angel!"

EPILOGUE: ONE YEAR LATER

I gather all the money I can, stuffing it into my panties and bra and make my way off the stage. "What the fuck, Dylan? I had at least ten more minutes in my set!"

Dylan, the club's owner, rolls his eyes as he lights a cigarette. "Gwen, you were boring the crowd."

"How fucking dare you—"

"Aye, watch your fucking mouth, or I'll take you off the books for a week!" I press my lips firmly together, crossing my arms over my chest.

"That's illegal, you know."

"And *you* know I don't like legal chat in my club." Dylan flicks the cigarette ash on the floor, giving me an annoyed look.

I smile, grabbing the cig out of his hand. "I see. I can only talk legalese when I'm getting you out of trouble." Dylan gives me a humorless laugh as I take a long pull. "Go figure."

Two years ago, I was at the top of my class at Georgetown Law, with dreams of becoming the best defense attorney in Washington, D.C. But then Dad disappeared after Mason threatened to break his legs. Mason had told Nana Rose that Dad's debt was her debt. Despite everyone telling me not to, I dropped out of Law School to help pay off the debt because no one hurts Nana Rose, not if I can help it.

So when Dylan's club was facing the threat of being shut down due to rumors of illegal activities in the secret "peek-a-boo" rooms upstairs, we made a deal: I would use my legal expertise to help him, and in return, he would allow me to work on the main stage at Dream Palace until I paid off my father's debt.

EPILOGUE: ONE YEAR LATER

"Ha. Ha. Funny." Dylan snatches his cigarette back. "Now go out there and offer a dance to some of Mason's crew. They haven't spent any money yet."

Fuck. I shift my weight from side to side, biting the inside of my cheek. Mason probably sent some of his men to collect the measly 500 dollars I pay towards my father's quarter of a million-dollar debt. "Come on, they love Angel way more than me." I roll my eyes, trying to count the bills in my hands quickly.

"Chop. Chop. You know you're Tyler's favorite." I roll my eyes, continuing to count. 15. 20. 25. Fuck, I only got 375.

I push my breasts up and take a deep breath, steeling my nerves. "I thought I was boring," I mock, sticking my tongue out at Dylan.

"Don't pick a fight with me. Get out there." Dylan points the cigarette at the door behind me, and I huff, sharply turning around on my six-inch stilettos.

I add an extra sway in my hips and make my way to the main floor, sliding just out of reach of some of the handsy men. I get wolf calls and "Hey baby," but there is one set of eyes that silently weigh on me.

I look up to the left corner of the club, my eyes locking with a set of deep blue eyes. His gaze burns into mine, causing a thrill to ripple through me. I can feel his eyes tracing every curve, every dip of my silhouette, as I make my way through the club. I am drowning in his bright blue eyes.

He holds my gaze and lazily sips the amber liquid from his tumbler. I lean forward, eyes hooded behind the rogue strand from his slick back, dirty blonde hair. I can't help but keep my gaze on him, his presence drawing me like a moth to a flame.

EPILOGUE: ONE YEAR LATER

"Goddamn, you are fine!" Tyler's whistle breaks the man's trance. I look up at the smug motherfucker in a white tank top and dirty blue jeans. His buzz cut is colored green but looks purple under the neon lights, and despite all the ways he could be cute, he is just shy of being good-looking.

I stare at the angry pink scar pulsating on his face, but I mask the shiver of disgust with a seductive smile. "Well, I heard you boys were looking for me?"

"Hell yeah, baby!" An eager member who looks a little too young to be in here smiles, looking at the rose tattoo that spirals up my legs and gathers on my left butt cheek.

"Come sit on Daddy's lap, Gwen." There is nothing more unattractive than a man calling himself Daddy. Major ick. That honor should be bestowed upon you, not self-titled.

"Oh, come, Ty. If you want to take me home, you need to try harder than that." I walk closer, almost between his thighs, crossing one foot in front of another, sliding my hips side to side like a snake charmer. Tyler leans back in his chair, legs wide, eyes hooded with a visible tent growing in his jeans.

"You know Mason won't let none of us touch you." I give him my best pout, squatting between his legs and peering up through my eyelashes.

Leaning up by his ear, I whisper, "Well, ain't that too damn bad." I'm not fucking Mason. I'm not fucking anyone, never have, but Mason claimed me as if I was his future wife. He knows if I had it my way, I'd have him swimming with the fishes before I would ever voluntarily call him husband.

Tyler swallows, his eyes running over the curves of my body. When his eyes land on mine, he licks his lips and says, "Jordan is waiting outside for this week's payment. Side door."

EPILOGUE: ONE YEAR LATER

"Thanks, love." I wink, blowing Tyler a kiss that makes his eyes lower.

With a flamboyant flourish, I turn around and switch my hips over to the side door when my eyes drift up to that man again. The tumbler he was drinking out of is abandoned on the side table next to his empty seat, glittering under the dance lights. I huff, blowing air between my lips. You need to get it together, Gwen; no paying attention to the hot, mysterious stranger's absence when Venom is waiting for payment.

Maneuvering through the crowd and keeping out of Dylan's sight, I make my way to the side alley. Knocking my right shoulder into the metal door, I stumble into the side alley where the midnight air bites at my exposed flesh. I gaze to my right, where Venom lazily smokes a cigarette.

"Venom, buddy!" I laugh, holding the metal door open with my hip and crossing my arms under my chest. "How the hell are ya?"

Venom, a big, burly man with thin lips and a bald head so shiny it gleams in the streetlights, smiles at me, flicking the ash from the cigarette at my feet. "Well, Gwendolyn—"

"Ew, not my full government." I grimace. Venom smirks, looking at me from the corner of his eye, and if I didn't watch him break my father's kneecap with his bare hands, Venom would be just my type. He is the enforcer in Mason's inner circle, and if I ever stopped paying my payments, Venom would be the one to track me down and kill me after he has all the fun he wants with me, and from his gaze, I can tell I would be in for a long night.

"From the tone of your voice," he takes another pull of his cigarette, "you're missing part of your payment." I cross my legs, giving my most innocent smile.

EPILOGUE: ONE YEAR LATER

"Oh, only by 125 dollars."

Venom lets out a low whistle.

"But I have three hours left in this shift. I promise I'll have it by the end. I mean, come look at these." I motion to my breasts with a clever grin on my face.

Venom finally turns his body to me, his eyes shamelessly ogling my chest. His smile widens, showcasing his pearly whites, while his eyes move from my breasts to the curve created by my tiny waist and wide hips.

I place my left hand on my hip. "Woah there, Venom. Keep looking at me like that, and I'll charge you."

Venom tosses the cigarette on the floor and places both of his large hands on my hips, dragging me into his chest. I yelp, scrambling to fight him off before the door closes, but I am too late, and he is too strong. "You know there is an easier way to work off that debt, Gwen."

"Oh," I giggle nervously, trying to wiggle out of his embrace, but Venom pulls me in closer, forcing me to inhale his stink of cigarettes. I almost gag on the smoke still spilling out of his lips. I make my voice firm, losing all of my playfulness as I make eye contact with his black eyes. "Venom, if you are looking for a lap dance, go inside the club."

"Baby, I don't want no fucking lap dance," Venom's smile is sinister, "I want you on your knees sucking my dick," he whispers heavily.

"Venom, what the fuck?" I jerk back in his arms, moving to knee him in the dick.

"You're right; that's only worth like fifty." His hands run from my waist, and he grips both of my cheeks, kneading my ass.

EPILOGUE: ONE YEAR LATER

"I'll fuck you in the ass after. We can call that an even 200, what do you say?"

"Mason will fucking kill you-"

"Nah, because you are going to be a good girl and not say a word." He pulls me in closer and licks my cheek.

"Venom, you bring your dick anywhere near me and I'll bite it off," I growl, slamming the heel of my stilettos into the toe of his combat boots; he doesn't even flinch.

"I always knew fucking you would be rough." Venom spins me around, wrapping my hair around his hand. He tries to push me down to my knees.

No. No. No. I can't lose my virginity like this and definitely not to a guy named fucking Venom. I dig my heels into the ground, using my body as leverage to keep me from hitting the ground, but Venom is too strong. My knees buckle, and I am left panting and praying to Gods I don't believe in for any solace.

A shot whizzes through the air. Venom jumps back, looking for his weapon, and tosses me to the ground as if I am nothing. "Fucking hell," Venom growls, searching the area for the assailant.

"I don't miss twice." A thick Russian accent rumbles through the air, but I am in too much panic to appreciate it.

The minute I hit the ground, I pat the area around me, looking for a weapon to defend myself. My fingers wrap around the neck of an empty beer bottle. I grab it, smashing it against the concrete wall and stumbling over to the other side of the alley, out of Venom's reach, brandishing the broken bottle as a weapon.

"When a lady says no, the answer is no." The silky tenor of the voice causes a shiver to run down my spine. My eyes lock with the same bright blue eyes I almost drowned in.

❋

Chapter 2

Gwen

With bright blue eyes, a man emerges from the shadow of the alley, caressing the pipe of his pistol as if it were a loyal dog.

Venom sneers, "You better fuck off before Mason has your fucking head."

Blue Eyes's lips spread into a sinister smile as if he was a kid playing with his favorite toy. "Oh, and this Mason lets you run around and rape young women?"

"Mason owns this city and everyone in it." Venom laughs as he points to me. "Especially her, so I'd mind my fucking business if I were you."

Blue Eyes shrugs. "You see, I would if she didn't say no, and well-" He winks at me. "When a beautiful girl says no to a jackass like you, I can't help myself."

It all happens in a flash. Blue Eyes reaches for Venom's gun, twisting his body so Venom's head is on the sidewalk, underneath Blue Eyes's knee, and his arm bent back so that Blue Eyes could easily break his arm.

Underneath the streetlight, I can see his slick back, dirty blonde hair, with a rogue strand dancing above his right eye, which is brown. I want to tuck that strand back so it can spring back and have a reason to touch him again. His blue eyes are vibrant and deep like the ocean, and he has swirls of

EPILOGUE: ONE YEAR LATER

intricate black tattoos peeking out of his button-up and up his neck. I swallow as my eyes land on the vein popping on the forearm that stretches to put pressure on Venom's shoulder blade.

When he looks up at me, there is a sparkle in his eye, and his lips are in an easygoing smile. "Normally, I'd break your arm, but since you were bothering the lady, I think it's only right that it is her choice what we do with you."

I twist my lips as if I am in deep thought because the idea of Blue Eyes breaking Venom's arm for me makes my panties wet. "Well, before you break anything in my honor, how about you tell me your name?" I purr, leaning forward to his eye level. Venom struggles beneath him, a slew of curses leaving his lips.

He brandishes a bright smile, rolling his name off his tongue like we are meeting in line at a coffee shop. "Nikolai Petrov, pleasure."

"Nikolai? Petrov?" Venom whimpers.

"In the flesh." Nikolai's cocky smile flashes in my direction with a flourish.

"Petrov, wait, I-I-" Venom begins to beg, but Nikolai clicks his tongue, silencing him.

"No. No begging now." Nikolai twists his arm, causing Venom to yelp, but he brings his eyes back to me. "Our handsy friend is getting a little impatient..."

"Gwen. I would shake your hand, but they seem full right now." I smile, flipping my curls over my shoulder, the broken bottle still swinging between my fingertips.

"Well, *Gwen.*" *Fuck, I love the way he pours over my name.* "What would you like me to do with the handsy guy here?"

EPILOGUE: ONE YEAR LATER

"Hmmm, you see, a broken arm can heal."

"Continue." Nikolai nods, intrigue flashing across his eyes as a devilish smile spreads.

"And I think this fucker needs a permanent reminder to keep his hands to himself." I purse my lips as if contemplating before looking down into Venom's eyes. "Don't ya' think, Venny?"

"Gwen, I swear to God-"

"Threaten her, and I will take your tongue as a souvenir," Nikolai growls, and heat rushes straight to my core. "Continue, love."

"Thank you." I beam. "I vote for a pinky finger, not too significant, but he'll miss it."

"I like the way you think, Kotik." Nikolai pulls a knife out of his back pocket, flipping it open. He looks at the hand he is currently twisting away from Venom's body, pressing the knife to the base of his pinky. He looks down at Venom with a nasty grin. "This may hurt a tad bit, mate."

The alleyway fills with the screams of Venom, and I think I am in love with a psycho.

Venom shakes in the fetal position, vibrating from the pain as he holds his bleeding hand. Nikolai looks at me with a mischievous smile, with the pinky in his hand. "For you, Kotik."

"How romantic," I deadpan. "Normally, men get me diamonds and dinner first."

Nikolai throws the pinky away as far from Venom as possible. "Those men are carbon copies of each other. At least you will remember my name," he teases.

EPILOGUE: ONE YEAR LATER

A smirk dances on my face. I cross my right arm under my chest and placing an inquisitive finger on my chin. "I'm sorry, what's your name again?"

He laughs in his low voice as he grabs my hand, kisses it, and whispers, "My name is yours if you want it to be."

My cheeks heat up, and electricity sparks where his lips connect with my skin. There is no reason for one man to be so sexy and smooth with eyes that make me so weak in the knees. The smirk he gives me while he looks at me through his eyelashes will end me.

"Jeez, you're too much of a charmer for your own good."

The laughter that rumbles through his chest causes me to catch my breath, wishing to hear the sound again and again. "And you are too beautiful for your own good. A girl like you should be throwing the tips, not dancing for them."

I pop my hip to the right, my nails wrapping around my hip. "What? You didn't like my dancing?"

Nikolai's eyes heat, his tongue poking out to brush over his lower lip before poking his inner left cheek and looking away.

"Oh my God, do you think I am a bad dancer?"

Nikolai's hand loops around my waist, his hand spreading over my lower back, pulling me into his chest. The motion startles me and I drop the beer bottle. The scent of leather and fresh rain invades my senses. His eyes flutter to my lips, the boyish smirk spreading across his lips before he makes eye contact with my breathless body. "No, my love, I love your dancing." His voice lowers. "I just would rather you do it in private for me."

I can't breathe. I can't think, not with Nikolai this close, and for the first time since the fourth grade, I fucking stutter. "W-well, i-if you wanted a d-dance. All you had to do was ask." *Jesus. Fuck. Get it together, Gwendolyn.*

His nose grazes mine. "Dance for me."

"When?" He slides his phone into my hand.

"Tomorrow. Let me take you out and show you the lifestyle you're supposed to be living." My mouth parts mindlessly, and I gather all the shallow breaths I possibly can as I type my number into his phone.

"Pick me up at 8," I say. Nikolai lets me go, and I immediately feel the chill of the night consume me.

He winks at me, not even checking if I gave him my real number, the cocky bastard.

Chapter 3

NIKOLAI

Gwen, my little hellcat, stands in a thin, skin-tight black dress adorned with sparkles in the bay window of the little two-bedroom house she and her grandmother Rose live in.

I am supposed to be here at 8, but I can't help myself from getting here early when all I could think about was her ass in that sparkly emerald green lingerie set with fishnets and neck-breaking heels.

She looked magnificent as she stood in an alley, with a cracked beer bottle in her hand and mouth too sharp for her own good.

EPILOGUE: ONE YEAR LATER

If she talked to me the way she spoke to half of the guys in that club, I'd have her writhing over my knee, her perfect bottom stained with my handprint as she begged for me to fill that filthy mouth of hers with my cock. I smile at the image of her big hazel eyes, almost brimming with tears, so turned on and frustrated with me that she curses my name, and I, in turn, punish her for it.

I bet she's a brat. *Fuck.* I adjust myself in my slacks as I stare at her, continuing to mess with her curly hair. She keeps fluffing her black curls, spilling down her back in spirals. They are more airy and free than they were at the club, swaying along her spine as she smiles at herself in the mirror. I keep flexing my hand in and out, waiting to thread my fingers in her hair and pull her into me.

I've wanted to run my hands along the curve of her waist, grip her hips, and make her feel what she has done to me since I saw her dancing. She had every man's eyes on her. Every man was fixing their cocks in their pants. Every man under her siren song, like the little minx she is.

She could be a modern-day Cleopatra, have men killing themselves just for a moment in her presence, and I could be her Caesar, but then I heard our modern-day Cleo speak, and she spoke like a warrior.

Men fawned over her, and she kept them where they belonged, kissing at her feet, so of course, when I saw that fucker try to rape her, I took his pinky. Fuck, I would have taken his life if she asked, but Gwen is a merciful queen.

I look at the time again: 7:55, which is early but a respectable early. I slide out of my Rolls Royce, adjust my suit jacket, and grab the bouquet of pink roses because Gwen texted me that *I better not be fucking unoriginal* and bring red. Bringing pink

EPILOGUE: ONE YEAR LATER

was a minor submission, anticipating when I had her on her knees begging for me.

I knock on the peeling white door. A pair of wide eyes and the slick smirk of an old lady greet me.

"Oh my." She fans her face, her eyes roaming over my body as I flash my most parent-friendly smile. "You must be Nikolai."

"Yes, ma'am," I say, kissing Nana Rose's hand. "And you must be Nana Rose?"

I wink at her, and a warm smile spreads on her wrinkled face. A gasp leaves her lips. "Oh." She points at me with her other hand. "You're good. I bet you're a charmer."

"Not as much as your granddaughter." I rise, smiling as she turns her body to the side, letting me into the small living area.

"Well, she got it from me!" Nana Rose claps. "Back in the day, I was a brick house. That's old lady talk for I was the shit."

"I bet you were," I laugh as Nana Rose's slippers click past me.

"Oh, I got the pictures to prove it! But make yourself at home while I see what's taking her so long." I nod, looking around the living room, cast in the soft glow of an aged lamp in the corner. From down the hallway, I hear Nana Rose call out, "Gwen, that man is fine, and he is waiting! Don't keep good-looking waiting!"

I look around, my curiosity about Gwen only growing as I take in more of her house. A pink and cream flower couch and a worn wooden coffee table adorned with colorful delicate lace doily sit in the room's center.

I roam over to a weathered brown bookshelf peeling tan against the far wall, its shelves filled with an eclectic mix of novels and a family photo of Gwen as a child sitting on the lap

EPILOGUE: ONE YEAR LATER

of a smiling man with a salt n' pepper mustache. I pick up the image, focusing on Gwen's wide, toothy smile.

"Well, shoot. If I knew you were going to go snooping, I would have told Nana to leave you outside." Gwen's snort breaks me out of the trance of the photo.

I return the frame and remark, "Consequences for keeping me waiting." When I turn around, her hazel eyes are hooded, her pink lips are glossed and slightly apart in a smile, and her hands are holding a small clutch in front of her.

She whispers, "Are there always consequences with you?"

Nana Rose comes back in, a slight squeal leaving her lips. "You brought flowers!" I hand them to Nana Rose as Gwen peeks at the bouquet with a smug smile.

"Pink?" Gwen questions.

"You said no red," I counter.

"And they are beautiful!" Nana Rose smacks Gwen's arm, narrowing her eyes at her before smiling at me. "I am going to put these in water."

As Nana Rose walks away, Gwen steps forward. The scent of coconuts and jasmine invades my senses. I swallow dryly, my eyes roaming over her now that she is in front of me. "Are you going to answer my question?" I arch my eyebrow, looking down at her. "You said that your snooping was the consequence for keeping you waiting, so I asked, are there always consequences with you?"

"Only when earned." I wink. She gives me a mischievous smirk, taking another step forward.

"Did I earn one?" she whispers breathlessly.

EPILOGUE: ONE YEAR LATER

"I don't know, can you follow directions?" Gwen raises an eyebrow, challenging me.

"*You* can follow directions; thank you for the *pink* roses." Her lips pop on the letter p in pink as she wiggles her eyebrows.

"I follow directions very well," I purr, pushing a curl behind her ear, watching the blush rise to her cheeks. "That's why I rarely have consequences, but the question was: can you follow directions?"

She shrugs, giving me her faux innocent eyes. "Depends on the direction." *Oh, so my little hell cat wants to play a game of chicken.*

I lick my lips. "Spin for me."

"What?" Her eyes widen, and she looks around the room.

"You said you would dance for me privately." I lean over to whisper in her ear, "So do it."

"I am not dancing for you with my nana in the other room." Her voice and eyes are firm as she pushes back, but when she places her right hand on her hip, my smugness reappears.

"I am not asking for my dance yet." I bend over so I am at eye-level with the scowl she dawns on her lips. "Just a taste, or don't tell me," I almost brush my lips against hers, whispering, "you're a brat who can't take directions."

Gwen's nostrils flare, but her eyes dart to the doorway her grandmother walked down in excitement. She takes a small breath, and I lean back, watching as she crosses one of her strappy black heels in front of the other and quickly turns. When she looks at me again, she pulls her lips into a smug grin. "There. Are you happy?"

EPILOGUE: ONE YEAR LATER

"No." Her brows furrow, but before she can protest, I whisper, "Slower."

"Nikolai!" she huffs.

"Call me Nik." I take a step back to see her whole body easily. "And I said slower."

Gwen bites her lip nervously, looking at the doorway again, but when her eyes land on me, they sparkle with determination. She crosses her heel over the other again, turning slowly, and I smirk, admiring how beautiful she looks tonight.

She's stunning in that tight strapless sparkle long dress, the slight slit in the back teasing at what lies beneath. Her big black curls tumble down her back, framing her face in a way that makes me want to mess them up. Those pink glossy lips, smoky eyes—everything about her is intoxicating.

Her eyes cautiously make contact with mine again, and she crosses her arms behind her back, accentuating her chest, as she sways from side to side. "So?"

"Fuck, you are gorgeous, Kotik." She blushes, looking away from me. I lean in again, my breath fluttering over the shell of her ear. "Tonight is going to be fun." Read Bratva King's Secret Twins Now Free With Kindle Unlimited and available on Amazon and Paperback.

ABOUT THE AUTHOR

VIVY SKYS the author of Steamy Contemporary Romance novels, featuring smart, strong, sassy and witty female characters that command the attention of strong protective alpha males, from Off limits, Age Gap, Bossy Billionaires, Single dads next door, Royalty, Dark Mafia and beyond Vivy's pen will deliver.

Follow Vivy Skys on Amazon to be the first to know when her next book becomes available.

Printed in Great Britain
by Amazon